# THE WITCH OF CRISWELL

# THE WITCH
# OF CRISWELL

## An Ariel Moravec
## Occult Mystery

## John Michael Greer

First published in 2023 by
Sphinx Books
London

British Library Cataloguing in Publication Data

A C.I.P. for this book is available from the British Library

ISBN-13: 978-1-91257-385-1

Cover art by Phoebe Young
Typeset by Medlar Publishing Solutions Pvt Ltd, India

sphinxbooks.co.uk

# CONTENTS

## CHAPTER 1

# THE EYES OF THE CROCODILE

Darkness rushed past the windows as the train lurched and rattled onward. Ariel Moravec, two days past her eighteenth birthday, tried to distract herself with the F. Scott Fitzgerald short story on her e-reader, but this once the glittering prose and Jazz Age setting couldn't hold her attention. The train was hours behind schedule, the car she was riding empty except for her: most of the passengers had spilled out the doors at the big city she'd passed an hour back, hurrying through the harsh fluorescent glare across cracked floors to the escalators and whatever unknown destinies waited for them in the city up above. The rest trickled away one or two at a time at little trackside stations where cars waited in half-lit parking lots and streetlamps went on one by one in the gathering night.

For the fifteenth time in as many minutes, she stopped herself from reaching for the cell phone in her purse and seeing how late she was. No point in that, she told herself irritably. If he's there, he's there, and if he's not—

She made herself stare out the window into the night, tried to guess from the dim half-seen shapes how close her destination might be. Reflected in the glass, framed in straight black hair cut shoulder length, her face stared back: cheekbones just angular enough to make themselves noticed, nose and chin

1

small, skin light and unmarred by make-up. Big brown eyes looked moodily at nothing in particular. A pixie's face, her mother liked to call it. Even before she'd gotten old enough for that to rankle, she'd hated the description, though that was mostly because of the lectures that so reliably followed it. Ariel scowled at the thought, then considered the expression. Were there surly pixies?

A streetlight off in the middle distance caught her attention. It vanished behind some closer darkness before she could see any of the landscape around it. A little later another light came into view, further off, and then more: scattered houses with yellow-lit windows, cars dotting the darkness with headlights or tail lights, streetlamps carving circles of pavement out of the unknown, a strip mall with gaudy illuminated signs above a parking lot bathed in blue-white glare. The leading edge of a tunnel cut it all off suddenly, plunged her back into night. Minutes passed and then the train shot out the other side. As it turned, Ariel could see the city in front of her in a blaze of light: a dozen midsized skyscrapers of Art Deco vintage flaunting bright windows against a starless sky, three lamplit bridges flinging themselves across the Shetamunk River, glare of streetlamps turning old brick buildings into a symphony of lights and fathomless shadows: Adocentyn.

Another tunnel swallowed the train moments later. The loudspeaker overhead cleared electrical phlegm from its throat and repeated the name of the city, followed by something Ariel couldn't interpret and didn't need to. She extracted herself from her seat, put the e-reader into her purse, and went to get two big ungainly brown suitcases from the rack at the forward end of the car. A conductor peered in through the door ahead of her, spotted her, left again without a word. Lurch and rattle, rattle and lurch: the train left the tunnel, curved along a broad arc, and crossed the river under a blaze of sodium lamps. By the time the other bank came near the train was slowing. It rolled on past another, slower sequence of brick walls and shadows, lumbered to a halt at the station a block or so further on.

The doors hissed at her and opened grudgingly. Suitcase in each hand, Ariel went out onto the platform, breathed humid night air edged with diesel fumes and shaken by the muted roar of the locomotive. A glance up showed her the sign pointing toward the waiting room. Blurred glass doors sighed and slid apart as she approached them.

Some train stations have their own distinctive character, but the Adocentyn station wasn't one of them. Worn black and white square tiles on the floor, worn wooden bench seats set back to back in rows as though leaning on one another for support, elderly brown-bladed fans hanging from the ceiling like thin-legged bats, a ticket office window over to one side with the lights on and a single weary clerk typing something into a computer: it could almost have been the station in Summerfield where she'd boarded the train that afternoon. The one difference that mattered was the tall old man in a dark gray suit sitting on one of the benches, who glanced up from a book, saw her, and got to his feet. Ariel braced herself and walked toward him.

"Ariel?" His voice was as deep as she remembered, and he seemed just as tall and gaunt as when she'd last seen him, though she'd gained more than a foot of height since then. Unruly hair, pointed beard, and great bushy eyebrows were silver, not the salt-and-pepper they had been, but his hands were just as big and angular as she recalled. Dark eyes, precise deliberate movements, jacket and pressed slacks and bow tie even on a hot summer night: it all brought memories surging back.

"Hi, Grandpa," she forced out. "I hope you weren't waiting all this time."

"No, I knew the train would be late."

"Oh. Yeah, I bet that showed up online."

He gave her a blank look. "I have no idea. Let me take one of those." He deftly extracted one of her suitcases from her grip. Her mother had chided her about that—"Don't let your grand-father take your luggage, Ariel, you know how old he is"—but she felt too tired and dispirited to argue the point.

"Shall we?" he said.

She managed a nod, went with him to the glass doors that faced the street.

His car, an old black Buick Riviera that looked as big as a battleship, sat against the curb half a block further from the river. They got her luggage stowed in the trunk, and then he opened the passenger door for her, closed it after her and went around. She drew in a long unsteady breath. Once he climbed in behind the wheel and pulled the door shut, she closed her eyes and said, "I just want you to know this wasn't my idea."

A moment of silence passed, and then the engine started. She opened her eyes again as the car left the curb.

A few minutes of driving got them through the bright lights and old storefronts of Adocentyn's downtown district, then past the old town green with the statue of Elias Ashmole on one side of it. She remembered the statue vividly from both of her childhood visits to the city. Green with two centuries of patina, the old archmage stood in the muted glare of street-lights, greatcoat open in front, wig spilling down over both shoulders in twin cascades of curls, eyes intent, lips slightly parted. One of Ashmole's hands held a tablet with words on it she still remembered, though they were in Latin and she'd never learned what they meant: VERUM SINE MENDACIO, CERTUM ET VERISSIMUM.

His other hand was raised up and outward, palm up. One afternoon when she was there with her parents—was it the summer when she turned seven, or when she turned ten? She couldn't remember—a pigeon lighted on it as she watched. It looked for all the world as though Ashmole was lecturing the bird, and she'd started laughing. Of course her mother demanded an explanation and met it with an irritated look, and Britney mocked her about it for days afterward: one more entry in a long and bitter list.

She struggled with her recollections as the Buick drove on and buildings hid Ashmole's statue behind them. From the old town green, she thought she recalled, you went eight blocks east toward the shore where the tall ships used to dock, and then a left turn took you uphill on Lyon Avenue past quiet clapboard houses and commercial streets, to where the oaks of Culpeper Park loomed up green and anarchic, blocking the right of way. Was that it? Her grandfather's hands on the wheel answered the question; so did the sign that announced Lyon Avenue. One by one, dimly familiar blocks of houses and shops slipped past, and street signs murmured names she almost remembered, until the Buick slid to a stop at the curb beside a tall house with green-painted clapboard walls and white trim, triggering a burst of childhood memories. At the end of the block the great dark oaks waited just as they had all those years before.

She got out of the car, didn't argue when her grandfather picked up one of the suitcases again, followed him up three familiar steps, past the wall-mounted mailbox with DR. BERNARD MORAVEC on it in gold letters, and through the big oak door. Inside, every last detail woke another cascade of recollections. "Let's get your things up to your room," he said. "Then I imagine you'd like some dinner."

"Please."

"Pizza? As I recall, you used to like sausage and extra cheese."

"Yeah. I still do."

He nodded, as though that settled the matter, and led the way up the stairs.

The room that waited for her was the same one she remembered from eight years before, big and comfortable, with walls papered in a pattern of roses against a cream-colored background, and a braided rug centered on the hardwood floor. A bay window looked out over the street and the roofs beyond it, toward the glittering lights and towers of downtown Adocentyn; another window, smaller, faced Culpeper Park. An ornate four-poster bed, a dark oak desk and chair, a big maple dresser and a matching vanity with a mirror completed the scene. The suitcases went over next to the vanity, Ariel thanked the old man, and he motioned toward the door and the stair beyond it.

Downstairs again, he called in the pizza order on a land line in the kitchen. She went into the parlor, settled on a big sofa covered with worn brocade the color of pine needles, and looked around at familiar furnishings. Around the walls, soaring bookshelves strained beneath the weight of hefty hardback volumes, more than half of them bound in brown or black leather and marked with faded gold lettering on their spines. Between the bookshelves, where windows or doors didn't take up space, curious framed tables and charts hung on the walls, full of dense type and strange emblems, communicating nothing to Ariel but a sense of mystery. A big black grandfather clock stood over against the wall to one side, with three dials: one that showed the time, another that showed the phase of the moon, and a third with seven hands that marked the movements of the planets. Further in, the sofa, three overstuffed armchairs in random colors well faded with age, a musical instrument that looked a little like a small flat piano with an off-center keyboard, and two ornate brass Art Nouveau floor lamps took up their shares of the carpeted floor. A long ebony coffee table in faux-Egyptian style occupied the center.

After a moment she looked up. Yes, the little wooden crocodile still perched atop one of the bookshelves, toothy mouth agape, gazing down at her with black beady eyes. That cheered her. She'd adored that crocodile, and gone out of her way not to pay any visible attention to it, since neither her parents nor Britney had ever noticed its existence. Knowing it was lurking there unseen, watching the room below as though pondering who it wanted to bite first, had cheered her through certain difficult hours.

Her grandfather came back in with a tray in his hands. "I hope a cup of tea will be welcome. The trip out here can't have been pleasant."

"No," she said, and then caught herself. "Yes, please, and no, not very." He nodded, put the tray on the coffee table; it held a Japanese teapot the color of a winter storm cloud, two mismatched cups, and a sugar bowl and a pitcher of cream, equally mismatched.

"It's been years since I last took the train," he said, breaking the silence before it became awkward. "I imagine it's not what it was." Golden tea splashed into one cup, the other.

"I think it was nicer when I was a kid." With a shrug: "I don't remember spending that much time sitting on sidings while freight trains went by."

"Still, here you are."

"Yeah. I'm sorry if that's a problem."

His gaze, unreadable, regarded her. "I was surprised when your father called me," he said. "We've never been close—his mother and I divorced when he was not much more than a year old, you know, and I saw very little of him after that. Of course I was at his wedding, but—" He shrugged. "A formality, mostly. And then the funeral." Neither of them had to say which one. "The two times you and your sister came here, when you were younger—I enjoyed those, though I gather your mother didn't. But I remember you from those visits as a quiet, pleasant, intelligent girl with a praiseworthy fondness for books."

"Thank you," said Ariel, past the lump in her throat. "That's—that's really nice of you to say that."

He nodded, acknowledging. "So when your father called and asked if you could stay here for the summer, he didn't have to make an argument for the idea."

"Did he say why they're dumping me on you?"

The phrase didn't dent the calm of his expression. "No, that wasn't something he mentioned. I was hoping you could tell me."

"They're taking Britney on college visits," said Ariel. "All over the country, Stanford, Dartmouth, Harvard, wherever. A road trip, doing all the tourist stuff on the way. Just the three of them, of course, and they couldn't even leave me at home. They're renting the house out for the summer, letting some stranger or other paw through all my stuff I couldn't pack—" She caught herself just short of tears, stirred cream and sugar into her tea as a distraction.

"You didn't go on college visits last year, I take it."

"I'll be starting community college in the fall," Ariel said. "Or getting a job if I can find one." Another shrug jerked angular shoulders upward. "Mom and I had a really big fight—this was six years ago. She told me that if I didn't do all the stuff you're supposed to do, I wouldn't get into a good college, and I told her I was okay with that." She gave him an uncertain look.

He met it with the same unflappable calm. "In my day, getting into college took decent grades, an application, and a modest check. I take it that's not the case now."

She shook her head. "Not a chance. Not if you want to get into one of the big name schools. You've got to take all the right classes, get into all the right afterschool things, have all the right opinions on all the right subjects, suck up to all the right teachers so you can get them to write letters for you, and it just goes on and on. Britney's at it seven days a week."

"And you're not."

Ariel shook her head again, harder. "No way. I told Mom I'd rather flip burgers and live cheap than do all that crap, just so I could waste my whole life working seventy hours a week for some sleazy corporation the way she and Dad do. She was so mad she screamed at me for like an hour." She looked down again, wincing at the memory. "But that's how Britney became the perfect child and I became Mommy's little failure."

The doorbell chose that moment to ring. Her grandfather got to his feet and went to answer it. On the way out of the room he glanced back at her and said, "What you're saying, I think, is that you want a life, not just a career."

She was still staring when he came back with the pizza. He ducked into the kitchen to get an ornate iron trivet, set that on the coffee table, put the pizza box down on top and opened it with a flourish. A wave of steam loaded with scents reminded Ariel of just how long it had been since her inadequate lunch in the train's café car. The old man motioned for her to help herself, and she extracted a wedge dripping with cheese. Before she bit into it, though, she said, "I didn't think you'd understand."

One of his eyebrows went up. "No?"

"You've got a doctorate."

"My Ph.D. was paid for by the federal government, back when I worked for an agency with a three-letter name. You'd recognize the letters."

She stared at him again, the pizza momentarily forgotten. "You were a *spy*?"

A gesture with one hand brushed aside the word. "An intelligence analyst, mostly. I spent twenty years working in an office building in Langley, Virginia, reading stolen documents from the Czechoslovak Socialist Republic and writing reports on their military plans. That was easy for me, since I grew up speaking Slovak with my parents and English at school, and so the agency sent me to Georgetown University to get a doctorate in political science so I had the background I needed. Then the Iron Curtain came tumbling down, everyone in my department was offered early retirement, I took it, and then went on to make some tolerably successful investments in Slovakian industrial firms with money I'd saved. Since then? Off the leash, you might say. For the most part I've pursued my own interests." He gestured again, indicating the slice of pizza in her hand; she blushed and bit into it. It was just as good as she remembered.

"Same pizza place?" she said when she'd swallowed.

"The same chef. It's only been eight years, you know."

She took another bite, let herself bask in the flavor.

"But I'm sure that's the other half of the reason your mother thinks I'm a bad influence," he went on. Ariel wondered what the first half was, but decided not to ask. "She wanted to know why I didn't go into the business world once I retired from the agency," he went on. "I don't think she appreciated my answer much."

"She probably wishes Dad was in line for a bigger inheritance."

He winced but didn't argue the point. Looking away, he extracted a wedge of pizza, bit into it. Once he'd swallowed: "But you're here and she's not. I trust you'll take advantage of that fact and have a pleasant summer."

Ariel managed a first tentative ghost of a smile. "You know, I think I'm going to try." The smile faltered. "But I have to call her tonight and let her know I'm here."

"And you'd really rather not." When she nodded: "Don't worry about it. I'll call her in a little while. She doesn't like to talk to me, so it won't take long."

"Thank you. Seriously, thank you." Another bite of pizza vanished. "You're being really nice, you know. Let me know what I can do around the house, okay?"

"Certainly, if you like."

"I don't know if there's anything else I can do, but if there is, let me know."

The old man took another bite of his slice of pizza. Somehow the movement reminded Ariel of the crocodile on the bookcase. "Who knows? Something might come up."

## CHAPTER 2

# A WOLF OFF THE LEASH

Something did, though two days went by first. Those were busy days for Ariel. She spent most of the first morning getting everything settled in her bedroom the way she liked it, with the six hardback books she'd brought with her—a matched set of F. Scott Fitzgerald's novels and short stories in light blue cloth bindings, the pride and joy of her collection—all lined up neatly in a place of honor on the back of the desk. Afterward, she learned her way around the house, from the dusty unused rooms upstairs to the spacious basement where the washer and dryer sat, not neglecting the rose garden her grandfather had in the back yard, with the strange sundial at its center, the pleasant stone bench at its far end, and neatly pruned rose bushes framing both in dark green dotted with flowers in a dozen shades of red. The only places in the house she left unvisited were the ones he'd asked her to leave strictly alone: a room off the basement that seemed to be some kind of laboratory, and his study, which was large and lined with books he didn't want anyone else to handle. By the time she'd finished her explorations, her grandfather was back from a meeting somewhere else, and shortly thereafter the two of them went out into the neighborhood.

Their first stop was the Culpeper Hill branch of the Adocentyn Public Library, a comfortable red brick building

11

with a tile roof and a bronze plaque by the door that mumbled something about Andrew Carnegie. Inside, windows in round arches spilled sunlight across long rows of black metal shelves loaded with books. The librarians there greeted her grandfather like an old friend and got Ariel supplied with a library card in a matter of minutes. Afterwards she and Dr. Moravec walked a dozen blocks or so toward downtown and stopped at the Heydonian Institution: a huge white marble building with fluted pillars out front and a soaring dome above, looming serene and patient over a neighborhood of old ornate houses like an elephant gazing tolerantly down on a herd of gazelles.

The big bronze door of the Institution swung effortlessly open when her grandfather pushed on it, letting the two of them into an entrance hall as big as a house. Lamps hung from a coffered ceiling there, a polished gray marble floor mirrored the light back from below, and a tall oil painting of John Heydon, the Institution's founder, stood gazing down from the far wall: a hollow-cheeked face with intense dark eyes, a great wig of brown curls cascading down around it, thin elegant hands, the ornate clothing of an earlier age. The walls to either side, flanking Heydon, had their own paintings: smaller portraits in gilded frames on one wall faced a vast canvas similarly framed on the other. That latter showed Heydon, Elias Ashmole, and a few other gentlemen and ladies in seventeenth-century outfits being led by a man in ancient Egyptian clothing to the door of a temple decked out in hieroglyphics, while three tall ships stood at anchor in what looked like the mouth of the Shetamunk River off in the background. Ariel pondered that and went on.

Her grandfather led her to a door halfway down the portrait-lined side of the hall. That opened onto an office, where a lean old woman with hair the color of polished steel glanced up past half-moon glasses, recognized her grandfather, favored them both with a fractional smile, and said, "Good afternoon, Dr. Moravec. Your granddaughter, I presume."

They got that settled, and Ariel sat down and filled out an application. Another precise smile from the old woman accompanied a card giving Ariel the right to visit the Reading Room. Her grandfather took her there next, and the two of them went through the leather-covered double doors into the echoing silence beneath the dome. A bald clerk in an ill-fitting gray tweed jacket, sitting at a desk next to the door, glanced up as they came in. He spotted Dr. Moravec and made a note in a book; the scratching of his pen was audible in the hush. Off past the desk, a dozen or so scholars variously dressed sat at dark wooden tables poring over volumes equally various, while two librarians moved noiselessly about. Dust motes sparkled in stray beams of sunlight, and wooden bookshelves dark with age stretched away into varied distances.

They stayed there only a few minutes, and then Dr. Moravec led Ariel back out through the entrance hall to the front door of the building. "So," he said. "Not everyone gets a visitor's card to the reading room that easily."

"Everyone there knows you," said Ariel.

"They ought to. I'm on the board of trustees." A shrug and a smile fended off her startled look. "One of the things I do to keep from getting bored." She rolled her eyes, he chuckled, and they headed back to his house, stopping for ice cream on the way.

The next day her grandfather let her know early on that he'd be busy all day doing something silent and uninterruptable in his study, and so Ariel headed out the door right after breakfast for an orgy of tourism. A double-decker bus tour she remembered from her first visit to Adocentyn started and ended across the street from Elias Ashmole's statue on the town green, winding through all the historic parts of the city in the interval: that was at the top of her list. Ariel climbed aboard the bus with a gaggle of tourists from a dozen states and three or four foreign countries, sat on the open top with most of the others, and listened to the young Cuban American woman in a bright yellow dress who narrated the tour. "Lots of people think of Adocentyn as an ordinary American city with a funny name," the woman started off, and Ariel beamed, remembering that same line from years before. "It's got the funny name, no question about that, but it's not really that ordinary of a city."

As the bus rolled and lurched away from the curb and started toward the waterfront, the tour guide told a story Ariel dimly recalled: how Elias Ashmole supported the royalist side in the English Civil War, how he'd had his famous vision at Lichfield after the fighting was over, and once the monarchy was restored, how he'd asked King Charles II for a charter to found a colony in the New World. The grateful monarch granted the charter, Ashmole gathered a band of friends and associates to join him, and three ships—the *Mercury*, the *Rose*, and the *Golden Cross*—duly plodded their way across the gray Atlantic in the spring of 1664 and landed at Coopers Bay, where the Shetamunk River flowed into the sea. There the colonists bought land from the local native tribe and founded Adocentyn. "Ashmole got the name of the city from an old book of magic," the tour guide said. "He was quite the scholar in that line. Astrology, too, which is why the colonists waited almost two weeks after arriving before they started building. They wanted to found their city at a time that would give it good luck—and you know, it seems to have worked." The middle-aged couple sitting next to Ariel put on sour looks at that, but she'd already spotted the religious jewelry they wore.

Once it left the waterfront, the bus wound through two neighborhoods on Culpeper Hill where most of the houses were of colonial vintage, neat clapboard-sided homes with little ornate porches framing their front doors and steep slate roofs above. From there the tour rolled past the mansions of the city's old families, festooned with many dormers, many chimneys, and neatly railed widow's walks where eighteenth-century shipowners once kept watch on the harbor. The Heydonian Institution came into view a little later, agleam in the morning sun. From her seat atop the bus, Ariel had a better view of the big marble building than she'd had the day before, and blinked in surprise at the words in Roman script high up, just below the green patina of the gabled roof: HEYDONIAN INSTITVTION FOR THE DIFFVSION OF ALCHEMY ASTROLOGY AND OTHER VSEFVL SCIENCES. The couple next to her put on another set of sour faces, but Ariel ignored them and kept looking.

She'd heard about the Heydonian Institution before, of course, but only in a dim offhand way: a place full of strange old books and strange old scholars in the state's oldest city, one more odd inheritance from as close to a distant past as America had to offer. Her visit the day before hadn't changed that impression much, though it had made her hope that she could find time to spend at least a few days finding out what the reading room had to offer. The thought that alchemy and astrology might count as useful (or vsefvl) sciences puzzled her, but not half so much as the realization that her grandfather was on the board of trustees of an organization with so curious a purpose. She shrugged and let those questions fade to the background as the bus lumbered on toward the north side of downtown and another flurry of historic buildings.

Once the bus circled back to Ashmole's statue and disgorged her along with the other passengers, she walked from the town green to the old waterfront along a street lined with bookstores and odd shops. She considered going into one of the bookstores, spotted half a dozen garish covers of kids' novels in the Bertie Scrubb series, still wildly popular that year; she wrinkled her nose and turned away. Another bookstore crammed with old volumes looked more interesting, but she decided to save it for a later visit and kept going down the street.

Once she got to Harbor Street, a little open-air seafood place called Captain Curdie's Fish & Chips on a pier over the water lured her, and she ate battered and fried cod and seasoned fries to the accompaniment of a salt-scented breeze and the splash of waves on the pilings below. Seagulls circled around the place and would catch the fries in midair if you threw them, which she did. From her table she had a fine view across the narrow end of Coopers Bay toward the working waterfront, where big skeletal cranes and container ships blotted out portions of distant hills and cloud-spotted sky. Memories stirred then, too, but they were pleasant ones.

After lunch she spent the better part of two hours at Duplessy's Museum, an enduring fixture of the Adocentyn waterfront and the focus of memories from Ariel's two childhood visits. It featured a fine range of lurid marvels, from two-headed fish and shrunken heads to the sword of the original Captain Curdie, a famous local pirate of colonial times, and a genuine Egyptian mummy gazing up serenely from its open sarcophagus. Next to the exit was a mechanical fortune teller, a waist-high box with a tall glass case atop it. In the case, as though sitting in the box, was a mysterious-looking figure in a hooded robe. Its face was hidden, its gender impossible to guess, and the one hand that hovered over a spread of faded tarot cards gave no clue to its identity. She considered the machine, then fished out some coins, set the dial to her birth date, and pulled the lever. The machine spat out a slip of paper that read:

> *You have come to a crossroads in your life. A possibility you did not expect waits for you, if you are clever enough to notice it. Danger awaits you in the west, but you will receive help from an old woman if you ask for it. Beware of pretended friends and keep watch for those who are not what they claim to be. Silver brings you good luck.*

No doubt it said the same thing to everyone who paid for a fortune that day, Ariel thought, but she folded up the slip of paper and put it in her purse. She looked in at a few other waterfront tourist traps and then spent another hour and a half at the Adocentyn Aquarium, where she watched the slow dances of octopi and starfish, laughed at the antics of sea otters, and shivered at the cold steady movements of a big shark in the aquarium's largest tank. From there she walked back up the slope to her grandfather's house, arriving in time to help with dinner. The expedition cost her a mild sunburn but left her feeling as though she'd wound up unfinished business from her childhood.

Pleasant as those two days were, they had their challenges. Getting used to a new if temporary home was one of those, and getting used to her grandfather was another. He spent many hours in his study brooding over old books, casting astrological charts, or sitting in perfect silence, and other hours in his laboratory downstairs, and they settled early on that he wasn't to be disturbed at those times. Sometimes, too, he played strange ornate melodies on the thing that looked a little like a piano—it was called a clavichord, she found out, and was tuned to some scale she didn't know—and then, too, he was not to be interrupted. The clavichord aside, the sheer silence of a house without a television was pleasant at first, after the constant droning noise of the media in Ariel's home in Summerfield, but now and then it got on her nerves and she put on earbuds and played something raucous on her phone just to break the stillness.

Then there were the texts from Ariel's mother. She got one of those each morning, no surprises there, with CARMEN MORAVEC-JONES right there on the screen just to make sure Ariel knew what to expect. The first one was a lecture on how she ought to behave around her grandfather, the second rattled on at great length about how she needed to get realistic and figure out what she was going to do with her life, and both ended with a flurry of prying questions she didn't care to answer.

Both times, as Ariel pondered the words marching in columns down the screen of her smartphone, she briefly daydreamed about snapping the phone in half and tipping the fragments into the little tin wastebasket beside her desk. When the urge passed, as it always did, she considered deleting the texts unanswered, but sighed and decided to take the safer course: type in a few sentences of bland generalities, make no response to the questions, and hit the SEND button. As she settled into bed on her third night in Adocentyn, hearing the low uncertain noises of the old house around her and feeling the prickle of the sunburn on her face and arms and legs, she considered the texts and the summer ahead and thought: I can do this.

The next morning she slept in longer than usual but woke with the familiar feel of synthetic fur pressed against her face. The fur belonged to a plush gray timber wolf nearly three feet long, which she'd gotten at a zoo gift shop on her twelfth birthday and treasured ever since. The wolf's name was Nicodemus. The fact that she still slept curled up around him had been her darkest secret for four years—girls in high school were supposed to be too old to sleep with stuffed animals, and she'd spent all four of those years dreading the humiliation she'd face if Britney ever found out and blabbered the news all over McKinley High, as of course she would. The day of disaster never arrived, for Ariel taught herself to wake early and hide Nicodemus in her closet before anyone else stirred in the house.

She rubbed her eyes, untangled herself from the wolf, and sat up. Through lace curtains she could see the shapes of Adocentyn's Art Deco skyscrapers glowing in the morning sun. All at once it sank in that she would never set foot in the bleak concrete halls of McKinley High again, and she didn't have to care any more, no matter what Britney said about her. That stirred a dizzying sense of freedom. She got up, straightened the bedclothes, and then set Nicodemus in his former place of honor at the foot of the bed, facing the door with his pink tongue lolling out. Once that was taken care of, Ariel threw a bathrobe for decency's sake over the tee shirt and panties she slept in, and headed across the hall to the bathroom.

When she'd showered, dressed in her usual summer wear of a baggy tee shirt and boy shorts, and read and postponed answering yet another long annoying text from her mother, she stood at the head of the main stair and listened for a moment. Her grandfather's voice came up from below, broken by long pauses. On the phone, she guessed, and headed downstairs to the kitchen, where she got toast going, poured herself a cup of coffee, and sat at the kitchen table.

It occurred to her then that there was nothing she had to do all summer, aside from the chores she'd already appropriated from her grandfather. She sipped at the coffee, and then drew in and let out a long shuddering breath, feeling the same giddy sense of freedom she'd felt in her bedroom. Nicodemus is off the leash, she thought, and so am I. Recollections of the unanswered text on her phone belied that, and so did the unwelcome memory of the trip she'd have to take back to Summerfield when the summer wound up, but she shoved those aside for the moment.

The phone call wound up, and Dr. Moravec came into the kitchen. "Good morning," he said. "I'm glad you're up and around. May I ask a favor?" She said something agreeable, and he went on. "I need to go out for a little while—half an hour at most. It's quite possible that some people will come looking for me while I'm gone. If that happens, can you let them in, tell them I'll be right back, maybe get them some tea?"

"Sure thing," Ariel told him, and he thanked her and left the room. Muffled footfalls and then the sound of the front door opening and closing followed promptly.

Time passed and the grandfather clock in the parlor chimed to itself, marking some interval of time that didn't have to do with the hour. She finished the toast and coffee, washed up all the dishes in the sink, and then went into the living room. The tall bookshelves tempted her. She went to the nearest one, slid out a big leather-bound book at random, opened it to the title page, and gave that a long uncertain look. The title was in Latin, and began with the words *Utriusque Cosmi*, whatever that meant. A long string of words she couldn't parse spilled down the upper part of the page from there, bringing her no further enlightenment.

Printed shapes of billowing clouds framed the title, and below them, surrounded in more clouds, was a weird image: a man spread-eagled against a circular diagram decked out with sun, moon, and stars. She paged further, found another diagram—a one-stringed musical instrument with a hand descending from heaven to tighten the string and the sun, moon, and stars marking off the frets, surrounded by complicated arcs and dense columns of Latin text. Shaking her head, she slid the book back into the open space on the shelf.

She had just started to turn away from the bookshelf when the doorbell rang.

The door had a peephole. It was at a height more convenient for her grandfather, but Ariel stood on her toes and stretched, and saw two people standing on the steps: in their forties, both of them, a light-skinned woman with blonde hair and an Asian man with a shaved head. She opened the door and said, "Good morning. Can I help you?"

They gave her startled looks. The woman said, "Um. Is Dr. Moravec home?" She had a West Coast accent—California, Ariel guessed.

"Not right now," said Ariel. "But he'll be back in just a little while. He said you can come in and wait for him if you want."

They looked at each other, but when Ariel stepped out of the way they filed into the entry. Once she closed and locked the door, they followed her to the living room and settled on the sofa. "Would you like some tea?" Ariel asked.

"Please," said the man, with the same West Coast accent in his voice. Ariel went off to the kitchen. She could see them through the opening that connected kitchen and living room, and watched them as she got the kettle heating, found a tray, and arranged the teapot and the cups. The woman wore a rayon dress in a garish red and gold pattern; her sandals had wide straps and flat soles, and her hair was pulled back in a ponytail. The man—Vietnamese, she guessed, thinking of school friends of hers whose parents had arrived as refugees after the war—wore a baggy button-up shirt and cargo pants, both in drab browns, and practical leather shoes. Married? Ariel guessed so, from the way they sat close together and the plain gold ring she wore. She didn't have to guess at their mood. They were worried, maybe frightened.

She brought the tea out, set it on the coffee table in front of them, and then perched in one of the chairs. "If there's anything else you need, let me know," she said. "Dr. Moravec should be back—" She glanced up at the grandfather clock. "—in just a few minutes."

"Thank you," the woman said, and poured tea for herself and her husband. "I hope he can help us. This whole business is—" She shuddered visibly.

"The people at the Heydonian recommended him," the man said, more to the woman than to Ariel, "and they said he's dealt with stuff like this before. I'm sure it'll work out."

Ariel nodded and tried not to look too puzzled.

"Have you worked for Dr. Moravec for a long time?" the woman asked her.

Startled, Ariel opened her mouth to try to explain that she wasn't an employee, but the rattle of the front door opening spared her the trouble. Dr. Moravec came in a moment later. The visitors stood up, introductions followed—the visitors were named Jill Callahan and Ben Thieu—and hands got shaken. "Thank you for being willing to see us, Dr. Moravec," Jill said. "Your assistant was nice enough to make us tea."

Dr. Moravec said something bland and pleasant, and waved them to their seats. Ariel sent a smile her grandfather's way and started to go, but he met that with the same raised eyebrow of amusement she'd seen on his face before, and motioned for her to sit down as well. Baffled, she perched on the chair again, folded her hands in her lap, and settled down to listen.

CHAPTER 3

# THE WEEPING GHOST

D r. Moravec settled into the big leather-covered armchair he favored, extracted a little black notebook from
an inside pocket of his jacket, and opened it. A thin
black pen appeared from the same source. He unlidded it and
poised it over the page. Ariel watched, and so did the little
wooden crocodile atop the bookshelf.

"So," he said. "You told me a little about your experience
over the phone, but it would be helpful to hear the whole story.
Why don't you start from the beginning?"

"Sure," Ben said, and drew in a deep unsteady breath. "The
beginning was that Jill and I decided over the winter that we
needed a break from the arts scene back in San Francisco.
Just—" He shrugged. "One of those things. We settled on
spending a year or two in an out-of-the-way corner of the East
Coast. A friend who vacationed here a couple of years ago told
us about this area, so we did some research online, got a list of
rental prospects, came out here in March, and decided to lease
a farmhouse a dozen miles west of town. It's out Lafayette
Road, a couple of miles this side of Norton Hill."

"The address, please," Dr. Moravec said.

"6115 Lafayette Road. It's a comfortable two-story place a
couple of hundred years old, just the kind of thing we wanted.
We visited it, we liked it, it has a room with good light for Jill's

painting and the barn out back makes a great studio space for my sculptural work, so we signed a one year lease right away. A month later we moved in, and—" He gestured and shrugged, palms up. "Everything was fine to begin with."

"One of the things we liked about it," said Jill, "was the neighborhood. It's very quiet, mostly little farms with a few woodlots here and there. The woman who owns the house, her name is Olive Kellinger, and she lives in a little cottage over on one side of the property—she's a widow, you see, and after her husband died she moved into the cottage and started renting out the house to tenants. She's a sweet old lady and keeps to herself most of the time. The two places on either side are both working farms, and one of them rents out the acreage Olive owns. Between her farm and the one to the east there's a woodlot full of old pines. If you keep on going west the farms stop and the hills start after a mile or so, and from there it's all pine woods for ten miles through the hills until you get to more farms around North Shadbrook. If you head back toward Adocentyn, after a mile and a half you get to a little place called Criswell, which isn't much of a town—just a post office, a fire station, a couple of businesses, and a few houses. From there it's farms for a dozen miles or so before you get to the outer edge of the suburbs."

"The names of the neighbors," said Dr. Moravec.

"Fred and June Northam—they live in a farmhouse just west of the place we rented," Jill said. "Bill and Dorothy Kellinger, in a smaller house a ways east of us."

He noted those down. "Relatives?"

"Olive's late husband was Bill's brother, I think," she went on. "And then across the road is Oscar Bremberg and a woman named Suzanne—I don't know her last name. His girlfriend, probably. He's maybe forty, and not very friendly at all. I don't know Suzanne at all, she moved in with him a week or so after we got there. She's younger than he is, and she has a bad scar down one side of her face."

The pen in Dr. Moravec's hand moved in quick bursts. "Thank you. Go on."

"We'd been there for a couple of weeks when things started to happen," said Ben. "At first it was just noises in the night, up in the attic or around the windows. Noises like footsteps—but not ordinary footsteps." He put his palms together and slid one across the other, making a brushing sound. "Like that. We both looked, much more than once, and never saw anybody. Then one night Jill woke me and—well, you'd better tell that part of the story, honey."

"I was asleep," said Jill. "And then I woke up but I couldn't move at all, and I was more frightened than I've ever been in my life. I keep a night light going in our bedroom, and I heard the sound of the footsteps and looked around and didn't see anything out of the ordinary. And—" The blood drained visibly from her face. "Something came into our bedroom. I still couldn't see it but I could hear its footsteps, getting closer, making that brushing sound. Then something dark loomed over me. I was on my back and I was staring up at the ceiling. All I could see was a dark place, and I could feel it pressing down on the bed and then pressing down on me, and all the while I couldn't move a muscle. I couldn't even blink my eyes. And I felt—" Her voice broke. "I was sure I was going to die. I don't know why I felt that way, but I did. I couldn't do anything, I couldn't move or speak, I just lay there, and then the thing was gone and I could move again, so I woke Ben."

"I was sleeping next to her the whole time," Ben said. "I didn't hear or see a thing, and then Jill was shaking me awake. She was really upset. I got her calmed down, and by then she was so tired she could barely keep her eyes open. So she went to sleep and I sat up for an hour or so, just to make sure she was fine, and then I went to sleep. As far as I know nothing else happened for the rest of the night."

"And the next morning?" Dr. Moravec asked.

"I was a wreck," said Jill. "I was so tired I could barely get out of bed, I had no energy at all, and I spent pretty much the whole day sitting on the sofa feeling chilled—and this was in the second half of May, so you know how warm it was."

"So I called my mom," Ben said. "I know it sounds silly, but my mom's really active in the Cao Dai religion—I don't know if you've heard about that." Dr. Moravec nodded, and Ben went on. "She knows a lot about spirits and stuff like that, and she's good friends with a Cao Dai priest who travels all over California doing ceremonies for people. So I talked to her, and then she called me back an hour later to tell me some prayers to say and some other things to do. She sent some stuff by express mail, too—we got it the next day." He looked sheepish. "I'm not really into religion, you know? But I grew up going to Cao Dai church, and I was spooked by what Jill told me, so I said the prayers every night and I taught her how to say them, too."

"More or less," said Jill, smiling. "I've learned a little Vietnamese from Ben's family but these are way past what I know. Still, I thought it was worth a try."

"Sensible of you," said Dr. Moravec. "Did you tell anyone else about what happened?"

They both shook their heads. "No, not a word," said Jill, "except to Ben's mom. I was embarrassed to talk about it to anyone else."

"You talked about it to Olive," said Ben.

"That was later, after the other things started."

The old man nodded. "And what happened after that?"

"We both heard the footsteps a couple of times," Ben said, "but whatever it was didn't come into the bedroom again. But that's when things started getting really strange. We started having little accidents: things getting lost when neither of us moved them, things falling off tables when nobody was close to them, stuff like that. We started having these weird bad moods, getting depressed or angry over nothing, and the only thing that helped was the prayers."

"And did you tell anyone about those things?"

"We talked to Olive about it," said Jill. "But that was after it started happening to her, too. She came over one morning in a state, you know? Pale and sweating and shaking. She was having breakfast and one of the plates jumped off the table onto the floor. She said—" Jill looked embarrassed. "She said there used to be a witch who lived near there, and she was scared to death that something might have made her ghost wake up or something like that. She was so scared she was practically babbling."

"I called my mom," Ben said then, "and she talked to her friend the priest. She called me back right away. She said that some evil force was working against us and we ought to leave as soon as we can."

"Did you consider that?"

"Well, to be honest, yes, we did," said Jill. "But we really love the place. Before this started, Ben and I talked about making an offer to Mrs. Kellinger and buying it if she'd sell, and we signed a one year lease, so we'd lose our money if we just moved out. So I did some searching on the internet, we found the Heydonian's website, and Ben called them this morning and talked to a really nice lady there. They told him to call you and—" She gestured, palms up. "Here we are. Do you think you can help us?"

Dr. Moravec considered her for a moment, then said, "Yes. Yes, I think I can."

They both looked genuinely relieved and thanked him, not quite in chorus.

"I'll need to make some preparations and do a little research," the old man went on, "but I should be able to come out to the farmhouse this afternoon, ask a few more questions, and see what I can do. Will that work for you?"

They agreed to that, and got to their feet as Dr. Moravec stood up. He extracted two small objects from his jacket pocket, and handed one to each of them. "For now, wear these, especially at night. They won't interfere with your prayers, and they'll help keep you safe. I'll bring other items later, after I have a clearer sense of what exactly the problem is."

They thanked him a second time, hands got shaken again, and he went with them to the door. Ariel's puzzled gaze followed him the whole way.

The door opened and closed again, letting in a muffled and temporary burst of street noise. Dr. Moravec came back into the living room a moment later. One eyebrow was up. "So," he said. "Did you tell them you're my assistant?"

Ariel blushed. "No. They decided that. I was about to tell them that I'm your granddaughter instead, but then you got home."

He considered that, nodded. "Well. I hope I haven't made too much trouble for you, then. I'm quite sure your parents must have told you any number of times not to have anything to do with the things I study."

Baffled, she shook her head. "No. They never said anything to me about that."

"Never? Well. That surprises me."

The question she hadn't asked on the night of her arrival forced itself forward. "Is—is that the first half of why Mom thinks you're a bad influence?"

"Why, yes. Yes, it is."

After a moment, she ventured the obvious question. "What do you study?"

He looked at her for a long moment, and then nodded once, crisply, as though he'd made a decision. "It's quite simple," he said. "My great interest in life is the side of things that usually gets called 'supernatural.' It's the wrong word, really—nothing that human beings can experience is actually outside of nature. It's simply that nature is much bigger and stranger than most people think."

"Okay," Ariel said.

"These books—" His gesture swept around, indicated the bookshelves and the old leather-bound volumes on them.

"Most of them are about that in one way or another. So are the books in my study, and of course the Heydonian has the world's best collection on the same subjects, which is why I moved here from Washington after I retired from the agency. That study has been my great passion since I was not much older than you are." With a little fractional smile: "No doubt you're wondering if I've lost my mind."

"No," she said.

Dr. Moravec went to the leather-covered armchair and sat in it. "No? I'm intrigued. Most people who hear me talk about such things aren't too sure of that."

She gathered up her courage and in a small voice said, "I saw a ghost once."

The change in the old man's face was subtle but remarkable. The raised eyebrow dropped back to its usual place, and the dark eyes focused on her with unexpected intensity. "Did you? Please tell me about it."

"This was at a summer camp I got sent to when I was twelve." She closed her eyes, let herself recall the details of one more unhappy time. "A place in Pennsylvania, on one side of a lake. One evening right after dinner I went down to the lakeshore by myself, to get away from some of the other girls. When I got past the boathouse I heard someone crying. I went to look, and there was a girl sitting on the edge of the lake, just sobbing and sobbing. I didn't recognize her, and the whole thing felt, I don't know, really creepy and wrong. So instead of going down further to say something to her I went back up to the main building and found Julie Schwartz, who was a counselor I knew I could talk to, and told her about it. She turned white as a sheet and told me not to say a word about it to anybody. Then the next morning at breakfast we all got told that the lake was off limits. The counselors said it was because of an order from the county health department, but they made that up.

"Then two days later a couple of girls I knew decided they didn't care, they were going to go swimming anyway.

They snuck down to the lake in the evening, and they drowned. Somebody found their bodies washed up on the shore the next morning. It was a big mess, there were paramedics and police all over the place, but a couple of days later I finally got Julie to tell me the story. The girl I saw down on the beach drowned herself something like twenty years before then. She got bullied all summer by a bunch of older girls, and nobody did anything to stop the bullying. So she walked into the lake one night. Ever since then, when anybody sees her crying on the shore, somebody else is going to drown."

"If you'd tried to speak to her," said Dr. Moravec, "it would have been you."

Ariel looked up at him. "That's what Julie said."

A silence came and went. "Is that what your consulting is about?" Ariel asked then. "You're a—a ghostbuster?"

Unexpectedly, he laughed. "Dear me, no. Not if you mean toting a particle accelerator on my back, or getting slimed, or any such nonsense as that. It's much simpler. It happens sometimes that people get into trouble with—let's call it the Unseen, shall we? With the Unseen, and they need help from someone who knows something about it and can tell them what they need to do—or, sometimes, do certain things for them they can't do for themselves. The Heydonian fields such calls tolerably often, and most of the time they send them to me."

"Wow," said Ariel, with wide eyes. "That's the cat's pajamas!"

The old man's eyebrows both went up. A moment passed. "When I was a young man," he observed then, "I knew old men who used that phrase."

Ariel blushed again. "F. Scott Fitzgerald is my favorite writer," she said. "I've read every one of his stories I don't know how many times. After I started reading him I got into lots of other stuff from the 1920s, and started saying the cat's pajamas, and the bee's knees, and twenty-three skidoo, and things like that. Everyone at school thought it was pretty weird but

they think I'm weird anyway, and the stuff they say instead—"
Her nose wrinkled. "It's really dumb."

"A young acquaintance of mine," said Dr. Moravec, "likes to
say that things are 'dank.' It took a year or so before I realized
he meant it as a compliment."

She nodded enthusiastically. "Dank. That's when your basement leaks and all the boxes end up full of mildew, right?"

"Exactly. Still, I can't complain. When I was young I used to
say 'funky' quite often, and that originally meant ill-smelling."

"You used to say 'funky,'" Ariel repeated. A little smile crept
across her face. "Did you have long hair and a beard back
then, and wear love beads and paisley?" He nodded. A stray
memory from an old movie came to her rescue then, and she
grinned and said, "Far out."

That earned another laugh from him. "Good! Yes, my friends
and I used to say that tolerably often too." He considered her
for a while, and she watched him and wondered what was
going on behind that unreadable face.

"Tell me this," he said then. "You have your driver's license,
I assume? Good. It would be helpful in certain ways to have an
assistant in this kind of work, and my clients already think I
have one. Would you be interested in helping me on this case?"

Ariel's mouth fell open. She swallowed, and said, "Seriously? Of course I would. That would be—" She stopped, fumbling for a word.

"The bee's knees?" Dr. Moravec suggested.

She grinned. "Groovy."

They both laughed, and then he went on in a more serious
tone. "If you help me, you'll need to do exactly as I tell you
while we're investigating, whether or not what I say makes
sense to you. I don't expect this to be a dangerous case at all,
or I'd keep you strictly out of it, but even an ordinary ghost or
magical spell or ancestral curse can be risky to someone who
doesn't know enough to stay out of trouble and won't follow
instructions."

The idea that ghosts or spells or ancestral curses could be ordinary was new to Ariel, but she took it in stride. "I'll do whatever you tell me to," she said. "I promise."

"Thank you. In that case—" He considered her again. "I'll need to do some research at the Heydonian before we drive out Lafayette Road, and I think it would be wise to make sure you have something protective with you, just in case. A colleague of mine has a shop close to the waterfront. It's an easy walk from here, or you can take the car if you'd rather."

"I can walk," said Ariel. "What kind of something protective?" Then the other obvious question came to mind. "And, uh, how much will it cost?"

"It won't cost you a cent. I have an account there, and I'll call. As for the other—" He considered her for a moment, allowed the faintest trace of a smile onto his face. "Why, I think it'll be best if Clarice explains that to you herself."

Ariel nodded, and wondered just what she'd gotten herself into.

## CHAPTER 4

# THE RAVEN AND THE KEY

Half an hour later and half a mile downhill from her grandfather's house, Ariel started along a narrow street a few blocks from the old waterfront. Century-old commercial buildings six and seven stories high loomed up above the sidewalks, squeezing the morning sky into a band of blue up above. Down in the brick-lined shadows at street level, little shops stood cheek by jowl, crowding up to the sidewalk's edge like horses drinking from a trough. Canopies in a dozen faded colors stretched out over the sidewalks, neon signs flickered and hissed, and here and there sandwich-board signs blocked part of the way, announcing deals by turns prosaic and cryptic. Windows at a dozen slight angles mirrored Ariel's image back at her in crazy-quilt fashion as she passed.

Halfway along the street was a store she'd been told to look for, an urban hardware store with signage that boasted of paint and window shades and wood stoves. Just past it, she stopped and glanced at the scrap of paper her grandfather had given her. The address on it matched a narrow shop front, with two neon signs ablaze behind the window glass. One of the signs, red, said OPEN. Another, violet and white, showed a staring eye surrounded by wavy rays, and below that the words:

AUNT CLARICE
CLAIRVOYANT
SHE SEES ALL

A fortune teller, she thought. Okay.

Before that moment, Ariel's only contact with professional fortune tellers had involved nothing more personal than staring out a car window at garish signs above little strip mall storefronts, on those rare occasions when one of her parents happened to drive her through the less fashionable end of Summerfield. There was a character in the Bertie Scrubb novels who was supposed to be a clairvoyant, too, but that recollection made her wrinkle her nose in distaste. She chased the thought away, reminded herself of a girl she'd known in high school who read tarot cards, and tried to convince herself that this Aunt Clarice couldn't be all that different. The effort didn't accomplish much, but she went in anyway.

The space inside the door was cool and dim, full of unfamiliar scents, and equally full of heavily laden beige shelves that looked as though they'd been salvaged years back from some other store. Along the wall to the left, which was bare brickwork stained with ancient soot, colored candles in tall glass containers stood in rows on a counter draped with an ornate lace cloth. All of the candles were alight: some burned steadily, others flickered as though stirred by an unseen wind. The wall to the right hid behind a tall wood-framed glass case full of oddities, among them the pale skulls of various toothy animals and an assortment of crystal balls on ornate stands. Shelves and the products they held filled the space between the walls so tightly that at first Ariel couldn't see any way through.

"Good morning," said a voice from somewhere behind the clutter: an old woman's voice. "Why don't you come on back."

Following that instruction turned out to be less difficult than Ariel expected, though she had to weave her way through shelves loaded down with little statues of saints and gods, candles in every color of the rainbow and then some, glass bottles labeled Florida Water and Van Van Oil, and much more. Finally she got past the displays to an alcove in back, where two chairs flanked a round table just large enough for two to sit at. A little counter over to one side held a hot plate, and a teakettle that muttered to itself in a language punctuated with steam. Cupboards up above it had moons and stars painted on them in little bursts of bright color.

In one of the two chairs sat a tiny old woman with deep brown skin, wrinkled as an old apple and fine-boned as a bird. Her hair, silver and tautly curled, cascaded back from a blue and gold head cloth; hands thin and angular as twigs emerged from the frills of a long-sleeved blue dress with more moons and stars on it. She smiled up at Ariel and motioned her to the other chair. "You're Bernard Moravec's granddaughter, aren't you? Ariel?"

"Yeah," said Ariel. "You're Aunt Clarice?"

"I am indeed, and don't you even think of calling me anything else." The old woman got up easily enough and pressed Ariel's hand with both of hers. While Ariel sat, she went to the counter with the teakettle, and busied herself with things from the cupboard above. "This one, I think," she said, "and green tea, definitely." She returned a moment later with a single teacup full of leaves and water, a saucer, and a bowl.

"Your grandfather tells me you need a toby to keep you safe," said Aunt Clarice, "but first let's see what you need to be kept safe from." She set the saucer on the table, the cup on the saucer, the bowl next to them, and then settled back down in her chair. Only when the old woman gazed into the cup did Ariel guess that the tea wasn't there for drinking purposes.

"You ever had anyone do a reading for you?" the old woman asked, her gaze still fixed on the teacup and its contents.

"I knew a girl in high school who read tarot cards," said Ariel, "if that counts. She did a couple of readings for me."

"Why, yes, that counts. Was she good at it?"

"Not really. She said a guy was going to ask me out, and he didn't."

Aunt Clarice nodded. "You've got to be gifted for the work. Not just in general, you understand, you've got to be gifted for the kind of readings you do. Me, I can't make tarot cards talk to me for love nor money, nor any other kind of cards for that matter, but the first time I looked at the tea leaves I saw all kinds of things, and everything turned out just the way I saw it. What I do most often these days is I look at the tea to know the past, and then I read the leaves to know the future. You'll see."

Steam rose from the cup into the quiet air for a moment. "Well," Aunt Clarice said. "I'm sorry you and your mother are on such bad terms."

Ariel reddened and looked down. "Grandpa must have told you."

A merry laugh answered her. "Good heavens, no. I'd be a poor excuse for a clairvoyant if I couldn't see that much. That sign out front? It's not telling any lies. Your mother loves you in her way, you know, and she wants what's best for you, but she doesn't have the wit to realize that her idea of what's best for you isn't yours and never will be."

Ariel closed her eyes and nodded.

"There was a big fight, five—no, six years ago, wasn't there? And something else before then, a year, maybe. I can't see it clearly right now, but there was fire involved, fire and pain and a lot of tears. Yours, and others too."

"Yeah," said Ariel, her eyes still closed. "I used to have an older brother. He died in a car crash. That was about a year before Mom and I had our big fight." She opened her eyes. "You're pretty good, you know."

"Why, yes, I know that quite well," the old woman said, with another smile. "There's good reason your grandfather comes to me to get readings for himself and tobies for his clients.

Oh, he's good at the things he does, better than anyone else I've ever met, and he's helped me out more than a few times too, but like I said, you've got to be gifted for the work."

Silence settled back into place around them. The old woman looked into the tea again for a while, and then started speaking again. "But since the fight there's been lots of cold angry silence between you and your mother, and not much else. Your father—no, he didn't want to get involved, did he?"

Ariel shook her head. "He never does, not when Mom's angry."

"Some men just can't handle women showing their anger, you know. Don't you dare marry one of them." Ariel looked at her, startled, but the old woman was still gazing into the tea, and what she saw there was hidden from Ariel's gaze. "If you do, you'll both end up miserable. When it's time for you to tie the knot, pick someone who stays calm when you get angry and holds you when you have to cry. But that's years away yet."

She glanced up at Ariel, then said, "Now let's see what the leaves have to say." She picked up the cup, swirled the tea around in it, and poured the liquid into the bowl with practiced grace. "Look here." She slid the cup and saucer part of the distance across the table. "The handle is your place in the cup, and what's close to the handle is close to you. It's also the south, and you can tell the other directions from there. The rim's right now, and the further down you go the further in the future you get. You understand?"

"I think so," said Ariel.

"Good. Now the first thing to look at is this line here." One thin brown finger indicated it, a thin unsteady line of tea dust a quarter turn of the cup from the handle. "A journey, very soon, going to the east. That ends in a fern." The little cluster of leaf fragments, Ariel thought, really did look a little like a fern leaf. "That shows you that you're going to be doing new things, things you've never tried before.

"Now we go a little further down, and there's two people and a cat." The little patterns of leaves didn't look much like either of those to Ariel, but she nodded anyway. "Those are people you're going to meet. One of them, maybe more than one, is hiding something—that's what the cat shows. Puss is facing away from the handle and also from the other people, so she's hiding it from you, but not just from you. See the way she's got her paws curled up under her? That shows you that whatever it is, it's been hidden for a good long time.

"Now look at the clouds over here." The old woman pointed to a patch of wet tea dust that did look a little like billowing clouds. "Those mean that you won't be able to see your way clear, not at first, maybe not at all. You have to keep trying—this line next to the clouds tells you that. You have to keep trying even when it doesn't look like you're getting anywhere, because there's a way through, and you just have to find it. And then …"

She stopped suddenly, and Ariel glanced up at her face and then back down at the leaves in the bottom of the cup. There were two little uneven patches of them. One of them, right in the center, was a thin bit of stem and a few scraps of tea dust that looked like a key. The other, over to one side near the clouds, was bigger and thicker, and looked a little like a bird with its wings outspread. A black bird, Ariel thought suddenly. A crow, maybe, or—

"A raven," said Aunt Clarice. She was staring at it, or maybe through it, with a fixed look that made Ariel uncomfortable. "That's a bad sign, a sign of trouble. Not natural trouble, you understand. When the raven flies, wickedness follows. Spiritual wickedness. Well." She paused again, then went on: "The key right at the very bottom, now, that's much better. If you can get past the raven, you can settle the whole business, and maybe something more. But it's got to be you who does it. See how the end of the key you hold is toward the handle? That means that you can take hold of it. Nobody else can."

She considered the leaves for a moment longer, then sighed. "That's as much as I can see for now. Now let's get a proper toby made up for you, and I can tell you a couple of other things that ought to help you."

The old woman got up, took teacup, saucer, and bowl back over to the little counter, extracted a tray from the cupboard, and then went over to the glass case and opened door after door, muttering to herself as she pulled things out. Ariel turned in her chair to watch. After a few minutes Aunt Clarice reappeared. The tray carried a collection of jars and boxes and bottles, and a little red cloth bag with a drawstring. She came back to the table, set the tray down, and sat in her chair with an air of satisfaction.

"Is it okay if I ask a question?" said Ariel. When the old woman gestured, inviting it: "What's a toby?"

"Why, something you hang around your neck or put someplace else close to you, to keep you safe. Some folks call it a hand, some call it a mojo, and over at the Heydonian they get fussy at you if you call it anything but an amulet, but my grandma Marjorie who taught me most of what I know, she always called it a toby. Let's see, now." She opened the little red bag, and then started unscrewing the lids of jars.

Her voice changed subtly, took on a curious rhythm. "Five finger grass, to stop any evil five fingers can get up to." A pinch of dried herbs went into the red bag. "Cocklebur, to break up a mess that someone's already laid down." More jars came open, and the thin brown fingers extracted a pinch from each, added them to the bag. "Those, no question," said Aunt Clarice then, still in the same almost singsong rhythm. "And what else? Vervain, John's wort, dill weed, yes, those will do, those will certainly do. And then black salt, good proper witch's salt. I get that made up special by an old lady down in Memphis, and when you hear me call somebody an old lady, why, you know she's got to be getting on there in years." She laughed her merry laugh. Ariel blinked, for the laugh had shaken her out of something that almost felt like sleep.

"And then?" The old woman's voice settled back into the odd rhythm. "A little Van Van oil, that's for sure, to give it power." An eyedropper dipped into a bottle of dark blue glass, rose out of it, let three drops of a golden oil fall into the open mouth of the little red bag. "And then a little something else, something special, to give it a blessing." Another eyedropper, dipped into another dark blue bottle, sent a single blood-red drop into the bag. Quick movements set the eyedropper aside, tied the bag shut, and fastened it to a loop of red cord long enough to fit comfortably around Ariel's neck.

"Now," said Aunt Clarice, and held up a finger. Ariel blinked again, and surfaced a second time from something that wasn't quite sleep. "Do you remember a single word I said about what's in the toby?"

Ariel opened her mouth, closed it again. The words blurred and twisted in her mind, and she had to fight her way to clarity, but she managed it. "Five finger grass," she ventured, "and cockle—something that started with cockle." One more fragment surfaced. "And salt. Salt from someplace—from Memphis." She reddened. "I'm sorry. I don't know what happened."

"Don't you be sorry," said Aunt Clarice. "Maybe you don't know, but I do. Most folks don't remember a word. I take good care that they shouldn't." With a sudden sly smile: "I can't have just anyone knowing what I put in my tobies, after all. But three things, that's good. You may just have a gift of your own." Before Ariel could respond, she held up a hand. "But that's neither here nor there, not now, not yet. Put this on and get it settled down under your clothes, right here." She patted her own chest.

Ariel took the toby, slipped the cord around her neck, and tucked the bag down in front under her blouse. "Like that?"

"Just like that. You won't need to wear that when you're in your grandfather's house, he's got the kind of protections there that nobody's going to want to mess with. But when you're outside, and especially once you're wherever he means to take you, keep it on you. I don't like the look of that raven, but the toby ought to keep any trouble from getting to you. That, and the couple of other things I mentioned. Now listen up, and listen close."

Ariel nodded, and put her hands in her lap.

"First." The old woman raised one finger. "Pepper in your shoes. Remember that. Any kind of pepper will do, red or black. Some people who do bad work, they'll put a mess on you through the ground or through one of your tracks, and pepper in your shoes will stop that."

Ariel nodded again, a little more slowly.

"Second." Another finger joined the first. "Silver. Remember that too. Keep something silver with you—and it has to be real silver, not just metal that looks like it—and if you think someone's trying to mess with your mind, you can touch it and break the spell."

"Third." A third finger rose up alongside the others. "This is the strong one, and it's not something you use except when you don't have any other choice. Iron. Remember it. Remember it in your bones. The kind of person who does really bad work, the kind that can't touch salt because it burns them—scratch their skin with iron, deep enough to draw blood, and that'll break their power once and for all. But you'll have your blood on their hands, for what they've done will come back on them, and that's not an easy thing. You understand?"

"Yeah," said Ariel. "Yeah, I think so."

"Now tell it back to me. All of it."

Ariel took a moment to gather her thoughts. "I'm supposed to wear the toby any time I'm outside Grandpa's house. I'm supposed to put pepper in my shoes and keep something silver to touch if I think somebody's doing something to my mind. And iron. Iron to scratch the skin. But only if I really have to."

Aunt Clarice beamed at her. "That's right. You'll do well." Then, the smile turning sly: "Do you remember what's in the toby?"

The words had vanished completely from Ariel's memory. "You did something to me."

"You better believe I did." The old woman picked up something from the tray, then held her palm out to Ariel. An old silver dime glittered in the palm. "Touch it."

Ariel touched the dime with one fingertip, and blinked. "Oh, of course," she said. "You said there was five-finger grass, and cocklebur, and—and vervain and John something—"

"John's wort."

"John's wort and dill weed, and salt, black salt, you get from an old woman in Memphis. And some kind of oil, Van something."

"Van Van oil."

"And some other kind of oil you just said was something special."

"That's right," Aunt Clarice said again. "Now I want you to promise me you won't tell that to anyone else." Ariel promised, and the old woman nodded again and said, "Good. Now take this and keep it with you, someplace safe." She handed Ariel the dime. "That's a proper silver dime, and minted in a leap year, so it's got even more magic in it than most."

Ariel thanked her, and Aunt Clarice said, "So that's as much help as I can give you right now. If you need advice your grandfather can't give you, why, you come right on back."

"I'll do that," said Ariel. "Thank you." Then, remembering: "The fortune telling machine down at Duplessy's Museum said an old woman would help me, and it was right."

"Oh, it is," said Aunt Clarice. "The Hooded One's good that way. It's not your ordinary machine, not in this town." She motioned toward the front of the shop. "You head on back home now. Your grandfather's going to be waiting by the time you get there."

Ariel thanked her again and headed for the door.

## CHAPTER 5

# A MATTER OF MAGIC

The black Buick was bigger than any other car Ariel had ever driven, and it wallowed like a tugboat, but she got it to pull out onto Old Federal Pike smoothly enough and joined the sparse traffic. Not far behind, visible in the rearview mirror, the towers of downtown Adocentyn jabbed up into a summer sky, glittering where the sunlight caught on their windows. To both sides, strip malls full of franchise stores lined the Pike, brandishing gaudy signs for the benefit of passersby. Little glimpses of suburbia splashed with aging paint showed and hid themselves in gaps opened by cross streets. Up ahead in the middle distance, the dim green shapes of rounded hills slumbered in the summer haze.

"The Heydonian has records of paranormal events in this entire region going back to the year Ashmole landed," Dr. Moravec said. He'd spent the first part of the drive guiding Ariel through Adocentyn's tangled streets, promising an explanation once they were on the Pike. "One of the first things I do when someone consults me is find out whether anyone else has had the same sort of trouble in the same place, or nearby."

"Like a ghost shows up in the same house," said Ariel.

"Exactly. The Unseen is surprisingly particular about place and time. So I spent an hour looking for anything unusual in the countryside west of Criswell, and I found something that

42

might be connected. Or it might not. Right lane—Lafayette Road isn't that far."

Ariel checked the traffic, guided the Buick over.

"One of the things our clients mentioned gave me a useful starting point," he went on. "They were quite correct. In colonial times, around the beginning of the eighteenth century, a witch lived near the place we're going."

Ariel sent a brief startled look his way. "A real witch."

"Very much so. Three hundred years ago, that's what they would have called Clarice Jackson, you know. Hepzibah Rewell, that was her name, was the same sort of person, the kind who could tell your fortune, treat your illnesses, take spells off your cattle, all the usual things."

That earned him another startled look. "Did people put spells on cows a lot?"

"More often than you'd think. You've never lived in farm country, have you?" When Ariel shook her head: "It's not the sort of mostly anonymous life you have in the suburbs or the city. In farm country the people you grow up with are the people you grow old with. That's pleasant enough when everyone gets along, but of course that doesn't always happen, and so you get grudges and hatreds that last a lifetime or longer. Too often they're passed down through the generations. And yet most often everyone has to get along in public for the sake of appearances. 'What will the neighbors say?' Those are powerful words in farm country, where your prosperity or your survival can depend on whether the neighbors help you when you need it.

"So there's always the temptation to turn to some secret way of getting back at the people you hate. Cursing their cattle, their crops, their children—all those are possible, and there are people who will do it if they can find out how. Sometimes you get cases where two or more families have been cursing one another for generations and all the malice and hatred and magic are knotted together in one vast tangle. Here's Lafayette Road."

Ariel had already spotted the sign overhead. She slowed, took the right turn cautiously, and settled into the more sedate pace the speed limit sign required. The strip malls fell behind. After a little while, so did the suburban houses. Beyond them lay a greenbelt of pines, and then a landscape curved and folded by time, cut by whitewashed fences into fields full of summer crops and pastures where cows gave blank looks at the Buick and went back to grazing.

"So Hepzibah Rewell, Goody Rewell as people called her then, had a reputation for taking curses off cattle," Dr. Moravec went on. "She also had a reputation for a hot temper, and there were people who said she was as quick to cast curses as to dispel them. If she'd been in Massachusetts or some of the other colonies, she probably would have gotten in trouble with the law, but here the colonial government didn't go in for that— quite the contrary, in fact, since so many of the leading citizens were alchemists and astrologers. So the witch of Criswell Village, as they called her, died quietly in her bed in 1723, and her grave is in an old cemetery just west of Criswell. For at least a century afterwards, people went there to make little offerings to her ghost for luck. For all I know, they still do."

"Do you think she had anything to do with what's going on?" Ariel asked.

"A good question to which I don't yet know the answer. She's the only paranormal item from that area in the Heydonian's records, so she's certainly worth investigating. But it may also be important that the Cao Dai prayers seem to be effective protections. To my mind, that raises some very intriguing questions."

Another patch of forest, mostly pines, rose up to either side of the road. Beyond the trees stood a little cluster of buildings— two houses, a Grange hall, and an off-brand gas station—and beyond that the road bent suddenly westward, toward hills less veiled in haze than they had been. Ariel slowed to take the curve, sped up again beyond it. "What's Cao Dai?"

"It's a religion. It was founded in Vietnam back in the 1920s, I think it was. Cao Dai is their term for the Supreme Being. A Vietnamese woman who worked for the agency at the same time I did was a believer. We used to drink tea and talk theology in a little coffee shop in Georgetown, so I learned a fair amount about it. That said, if any form of prayer can chase something off—"

He glanced out the window. "Ah. I'll need a little silence. We're close."

Ariel nodded, drove on without saying more. The land rose and fell in slow curves around the road. Fields, woodlots, and farmhouses slipped past, drowsing in hazy sunlight. Mailboxes on wooden posts by the roadside at driveways' ends, each marked with the house number, gave her what guidance she needed. Another little clutch of buildings appeared in the distance ahead: Criswell, she guessed, and was rewarded a mile or so later by signs on two bland little brick buildings, announcing the Criswell Post Office and the Criswell Fire Department. Those and the clutch of houses and businesses around them soon vanished into the distance behind, and Ariel drove on.

All the while, her grandfather sat in the passenger seat, his eyes closed and his hands folded in his lap, his face calm but intent. He looked, Ariel thought, as though he was listening to something she couldn't hear. She drove on, thinking about the weird experiences she'd had at Aunt Clarice's shop, then about the things Dr. Moravec had told her about Hepzibah Rewell, the witch of Criswell Village, and then about the toby around her neck, the silver dime in her purse, and the pepper she'd sprinkled in each of her shoes before they'd gotten into the Buick.

Witches, ghosts, magic: those weren't supposed to be real. She knew that well enough. The science teacher she'd had in middle school who made a little speech mocking people who talked about ESP and flying saucers, the little circle of boys she'd known in high school who liked to call themselves skeptics and start arguments with anyone who believed something they didn't like, the talking heads on television programs saying the same things in a hundred different ways—oh, she'd had any number of run-ins with people like that, and learned to keep her mouth shut about anything that might make her a target for their mockery or their anger. That was as far as she would bend, though. All their bluster couldn't erase the terrible memory of a summer evening in the Pennsylvania woods, the huddled figure sobbing by the water's edge, the tremendous sense of wrongness gathering in the fading light.

Fields went by to both sides, then a mailbox with the name KELLINGER stenciled on it and the number 6070 below that. It marked the driveway of an old rundown farmhouse a short distance from the road. The roof was patched and the faded blue paint peeled in places. The big barn behind it, painted the same color as the house, looked just as run-down. More fields slid by, half a mile or so in all. Then the Buick passed a woodlot thick with old bent pines and approached a loose cluster of three houses, two on the right side of the road and one on the left.

The one to the left was a gray split-level place with deep eaves that looked like it belonged in a postwar suburb. It was set only a little back from the road, with a separate two-car garage close by, and tall ornamental yews in long lines against the road to either side. On the right, up a driveway, was a house that looked centuries older: a comfortable clapboard-sided farmhouse of two stories, painted white, with a small porch out front, narrow windows, a big brick chimney rising out of the center of the gambrel roof, and a white-painted barn further off. A whitewashed board fence ran along the roadside, sporting a sign that said HORSES BOARDED with a phone number beneath it. The fence gapped once for the driveway, and the mailbox that stood next to the gap was marked KELLINGER 6115.

A quarter mile or so further west stood another house on a driveway of its own. It was a tall narrow nineteenth-century place, dull brown in color, with a porch wrapping around two sides. Only as Ariel slowed to make the turn into the Kellinger driveway did she also see the little cottage past the white barn, up against the woodlot, its sides a cheerful red with white trim.

The driveway of the Kellinger farm ran more or less straight to a shapeless open area in front of the house, where a blue Nissan hybrid with California plates was parked. Ariel saw that and the house number above the porch at a single glance, let out a little sigh of relief that she'd gotten to the right place, and parked the Buick next to the Nissan.

Dr. Moravec opened his eyes as soon as the Buick's engine stopped. "Thank you," he said. "That was quite helpful. Any questions before we go in?"

"Nope," said Ariel. They'd talked over what he wanted her to do before they'd headed for the Buick. He smiled and motioned with his head, and Ariel nodded in response and opened the door on her side.

A mixture of familiar and unfamiliar scents made a chorus on the breeze as she got out of the car: resin blowing past from the pines in the woodlot, hay and animal scents from the barn, dust and sun-warmed metal from closer by, with warm earth sounding a bass note beneath them all. She closed the door, waited for her grandfather to get out and extract a brown leather valise from behind his seat. Once he closed the door she followed him up to the porch. As they walked, a black shape detached itself from the roof and flew off with heavy wing strokes, letting out a dismal croaking sound. Ariel pivoted to watch it, recognized it: a raven, a big one.

Ben Thieu opened the door a moment later. He had a cheerful smile on, but Ariel could see through it easily enough and sense the worries underneath. She waited while he and her grandfather exchanged pleasantries, followed them inside. The entry was a square white-plastered space with a stair rising up across the far wall to the story above, and glass-paned doors to either side. The one on the left opened onto a comfortably furnished parlor, also in white plaster, with a big brick fireplace not far from the door, rural-themed paintings on the walls, and windows divided into little square panes, looking out in three directions across the landscape.

Jill Callahan got up from a chair when they came through the door. She wore a smile of her own, more fragile than her husband's, but she looked just as frightened underneath it.

"Thank you for coming," she said.

"You're most welcome," said Dr. Moravec. "I gather things have gotten worse."

"Yeah," said Ben after a moment. "Did you sense that?"

"From your expressions. Why don't you tell me what's happened, and then we can talk about the next steps."

Ben nodded and sat down in a well-worn armchair, and Jill settled in another. Dr. Moravec sat on one side of a long brocade-covered couch. Ariel perched on the other end, got out her phone, opened a text file, and waited.

"Well, the things you gave us helped in one way," Ben said. "I said something about us getting depressed or angry for no reason, and getting into fights, right? That stopped cold as soon as we put them on. It was like walking out of a dark stuffy place into sunlight and fresh air." He gestured, palms up. "So that was good. The problem is that the rest of it's gotten a lot worse. We were having lunch in the kitchen and a plate slid across the table and fell onto the floor and broke. I swear I'm not making that up. I got up and tried to catch it but it happened too fast. Four pictures have fallen off the walls, and the nails didn't come loose—something pushed the wires off them. We've heard thumps and bangs from I don't know where, and a couple of times something that sounded like a rock hitting the side of the house from outside. And—" The last traces of his smile trickled away. "There's something else. Like—pressure. Something pushing against us."

Ariel finished typing in a quick summary, glanced at her grandfather.

"I felt it before we arrived," said Dr. Moravec calmly. "It's quite clear that something or someone wants the two of you out of this house, and very likely off the property as well. I assume you still intend to stay."

They both nodded. "Maybe we're just stubborn," said Ben, "but we talked about it on the way back from visiting you and decided we're staying. I can't speak for Jill but I'll be damned if I'm going to let a bunch of noises chase us out of here." He glanced at his wife, who nodded once, a crisp sharp nod that didn't need words to interpret it.

"In that case," Dr. Moravec said, "the first priority is to clear away the negative energies from the house and keep them from getting reestablished. That's easy enough to do, and shouldn't take long. The second priority is finding out who or what is behind all this, and why. That's a little more difficult, and will very likely take longer. Now." He held up one finger. "Does this house have a cellar?"

"Yes," said Ben. "I can take you down there if you want."

"In a few minutes." He held up a second finger. "How many doors let into the cellar, and can you lock them?"

Ben looked puzzled. "Just one, and yes, it's got a lock on it."

"Who has access to the key?"

"It's on a hook in the broom closet," said Jill. "That's the only copy."

"Your landlady doesn't have one?"

She shook her head. "She said there's just the one."

Dr. Moravec took hold of the valise, and stood up. "Perhaps you can show me the cellar now. Ariel, you'll want to come with us."

Ben led the way into the kitchen, a big spacious room with wide counters, old appliances, and a tile floor, all of it spotlessly clean. He went to the broom closet, got the key, and used it to open an inconspicuous door off past the refrigerator. That let onto a narrow stairway of brown-painted wood that slanted down into darkness. A switch clicked on, waking a bare bulb further down. By that harsh light they descended single file into a cluttered, echoing space.

The walls were mortared stone, the floor was covered with flat gray flagstones, and the ceiling showed bare beams with insulation batts between them and a few light fixtures nailed in place, each with its own bare bulb. An old washer and dryer stood against one wall, next to an angular galvanized laundry sink. The foundations of the chimney filled the center, with a modern furnace and hot water heater gathered close by. Up against the far wall stood a workbench a dozen feet long with shallow shelves above it festooned with jars full of screws and nails and spare parts. Elsewhere, an impressive array of clutter pressed against the walls: gardening tools, rusty washtubs, steamer trunks, two old vacuum cleaners, a wooden crate nearly the size of a coffin with arrows marked THIS END UP pointing straight to the floor, a couple of full-length mirrors with next to no silvering left, and much more.

"Excellent," said Dr. Moravec. "I'll need to get into the four corners, and then it would be very helpful if things could be moved to keep anyone else from getting to them."

Ben gave him a startled look, and then said, "Okay. I can do that."

The two of them went to the nearest corner, and moved just enough of the clutter to let Dr. Moravec through. The old man opened his valise, took something out of it, and bent to set it on the floor. Once he finished and stepped back, he and Ben moved everything back and then hefted a steamer trunk on top of the clutter that was already there.

By the time they moved to the next corner Ariel went to help, and did her share of lifting and carrying. When they got to the third corner she was able to catch a glimpse of what her grandfather put there: a flat square piece of gray metal that had a complex pattern of lines and letters graven into it. That got clutter heaped on top of it, and so did an identical object in the fourth corner, up underneath one end of the workbench.

"And there we are," said Dr. Moravec then. He walked over to the middle of the cellar, next to the base of the chimney, raised both hands, and in a low voice said something in a language Ariel didn't know.

The effect was instant. Like walking out of a dark stuffy place into sunlight and fresh air: Ben could have been describing that moment, Ariel thought. Then it occurred to her that she hadn't noticed just how oppressive the farmhouse had felt until then.

"Wow," said Ben, and Jill: "That's quite a change."

"Thank you," said Dr. Moravec. "Now I have certain things to suggest. The first is that once we go back upstairs, the door should be locked, and one of you should take the key and put it in a safe place. It mustn't go back into the broom closet, or anywhere that someone might be likely to look. If it can be kept under lock and key, that would be best. Can you do that?"

That earned him startled looks from Ben and Jill, but after a moment Ben said, "Yes. I've got a filing cabinet upstairs with a lock on it. I can stick the key in one of the file folders."

"That will do very well. The second is that nobody but the four of us should know why Ariel and I came here. Would you mind telling anyone who asks that we're relatives, say?"

"Sure," said Jill. "My relatives, obviously—but you can be my Uncle Bernard and your assistant—"

"Ariel," Dr. Moravec said. "We have the same last name, if that's helpful."

"Cousin Ariel it is," said Jill, with a smile she didn't have to force.

Ariel smiled back at her. "Excellent," said Dr. Moravec. "My third suggestion is that if anyone tries to get access to the cellar, or asks more than casual social questions about Ariel or me, call me at once."

"Why—" Ben started, and then stopped. His eyebrows moved closer together.

"Exactly," Dr. Moravec said. "The disturbances here might be the work of a disembodied being but they might also be the work of a living person. If it's the latter, their first priority will be to come down here and try to remove the protective talismans I've just placed, and their second priority will be to find out who placed them. Once they show themselves, why, then we can decide the next step, if a next step is needed."

"Okay," said Ben, and Jill repeated the word a moment later.

"Thank you. The fourth is much simpler. It's just possible that I may be able to sense who or what is behind all this trouble. If you can lend me a private room with a chair, and let's say an hour of uninterrupted quiet, I'll make the attempt."

"There's an office upstairs," said Jill, "with an armchair. You can certainly use that."

"Thank you." He turned to Ariel. "While I'm doing that, perhaps you can walk around the property and see what you can perceive." To the others: "Maybe one of you can show her around, if that's not too much trouble."

"No trouble at all," Jill said.

CHAPTER 6

# THE CURSE OF THE KELLINGERS

Outside the afternoon had gotten hotter and hazier. The wind had fallen away to stillness, letting the smells from the barn pool and turn rank, while the pines in the woodlot flooded the air with resin as they drowsed. Somewhere in the middle distance, a tractor cleared its throat and came to life. The sound of its engine faded as it headed off to its labors.

"Two horses," said Jill as she and Ariel crossed the yard to the big white barn. "Olive makes some money boarding horses for people who live in town. She's got a girl named Ricky who lives a couple of miles up the road, and comes in twice a day to take care of them. I ride them whenever I have the time. I took riding lessons when I was younger, so I know how."

Ariel wrestled down a burst of frantic jealousy, and nodded.

"Let's see. A bunch of barn cats to keep the rats under control, sort of, and a barn owl—nobody owns him, Olive says he just showed up one day. The cows you'll see in the pasture over that way—" She gestured west toward the hills. "They belong to the Northams. No chickens, unfortunately. If we buy this place I'm getting some."

"You like chickens?"

"I grew up with chickens," said Jill. "My mom and dad were living in a commune up by Mount Shasta when they had me, and I was eight before the commune finally ran out of money and they had to sell the land and move back into town. By the time I was three I was picking slugs out of the garden and tossing them to the chickens to eat."

"Ew," said Ariel.

"Oh, I know. But when you're three you don't care how slimy they are." They reached the barn door, and Jill hauled on it until it came partway open. Scents of hay and horses swept outward with nearly tangible force. What Ariel saw first, however, were big ragged pieces of pale gray stone lying on the ground, more than a dozen of them, the smallest larger than her head and the biggest more than four feet long and two feet or so wide and thick. They lay scattered as though someone had flung them there at random.

"This is Ben's studio," Jill said. "Or half of it. He hauls the pieces out into the barnyard when he wants to use power tools, because the horses don't like the noise."

She hauled the barn door shut behind them, and the two of them picked their way around the stones through the still air and deep shadows of the barn. One of the barn cats, a big orange tom perched on a partition beyond the studio, glanced incuriously at them and then turned its attention back to something in front of it that Ariel couldn't see. She looked up, and drew in a sudden sharp breath as she spotted the white ghost-face of the owl past the hayloft up above.

Jill noticed the breath, glanced at her and then up at the owl. "Yes, that's Barney," she said. "That's what we call him. Unoriginal, I know."

They passed two rusty International tractors that both looked long past any hope of repair, then a long row of empty stalls, and finally reached the two horses, not far from the barn's other end. One was a big gray gelding, the other a smaller chestnut mare with an uneven white star on her forehead. The gray whickered at Jill as she came into sight, and both of them came to the front of their stalls and waited expectantly.

"You two are spoiled rotten," Jill told them, but crossed to a bin, over by the wall where saddles lay across a beam and tack hung on iron hooks, and brought back a pair of big woody carrots. She handed one of them to Ariel. "Give this to Corazon and she'll love you forever," she said, indicating the mare with a motion of her head. "Stormalong here is a bit of a bully so you probably ought to leave him to me."

Ariel thanked her and went over to the mare's stall. Corazon turned her head to one side to get a good look at Ariel, then crunched up the carrot with every sign of enthusiasm and bent her neck to let Ariel stroke her muzzle. Meanwhile Jill kept up her end of a conversation with the gelding, who took the other carrot and then tossed his head, whickered again, and finally accepted a pat on the nose.

"So," said Jill as they went out the doors in the far end of the barn, into another yard where the ground had long since been pounded into dust by hooves. "Straight ahead is the pasture for the horses. They were out in the morning and they'll be out again for exercise once the heat breaks—Ricky's really good about making sure they're comfortable. Further off the same direction and then off that way—" She gestured to the left. "That's all Olive's property, but Fred Northam rents it and farms it. The Northams own the fields north of their house, that's the brown one, and then a lot of acreage on the other side of the road."

Ariel looked westward, toward the Northams' house. She could see a woman in a blue sun dress standing on the porch. Was she watching the Kellinger house and barn? From a quarter mile, Ariel couldn't be sure, but it looked that way.

"Then off that way," Jill began, and stopped. "Oh, hi, Olive."

Ariel turned. A plump old woman in a pleasant green dress and a white cardigan was coming toward them. Her face was wrinkled and smiling and her hair had almost finished changing from gray to white; she had big round glasses that made her eyes, which were light blue, look much larger than they were; she had a cane in her left hand, but walked briskly, as though she could readily do without it. Watching her, Ariel found herself hoping that she could be that smiling and active when she got old.

"Good afternoon," the old woman said. "I don't think I've met your friend yet, Jill."

"My cousin Ariel," said Jill. "Uncle Bernard drove here today to pay a surprise visit. Ariel's his granddaughter."

"Why, then, I'm very pleased to meet you," the old woman said, and pressed Ariel's hand with hers. "In case Jill hasn't gotten around to telling you yet, I'm Olive Kellinger."

"Nice to meet you," said Ariel.

"I was showing her around the place," Jill said. "I'm pretty sure she's never had the chance to visit a working farm before."

"Nope." Ariel made a face. "I grew up in the suburbs."

"Why, better late than never." The old woman beamed impartially at them both. "Though it's not half the farm it was when my husband Glen was still with us. You've been to see the horses, I hope? Oh, good. Aside from that and the pasture there's not much left."

"There's the woodlot," said Jill. "I wanted to take her over to that, too."

The smile on Mrs. Kellinger's face faltered, though it didn't quite vanish. "Oh, I wish you wouldn't. I know you probably think I'm just a silly old woman with a head full of old stories, but it's not lucky to get too close to that, not lucky at all. I think somebody might have gone in there, you know, and I wonder if maybe that might be behind—" She stopped abruptly.

"I've told Ariel what's happened," said Jill.

Mrs. Kellinger looked relieved. "Why, that's probably just as well." To Ariel: "I don't imagine you believe in witches."

Two things occurred to Ariel at that moment. The first was that she might be able to learn something useful from the old woman; the second was that telling the truth might be a good way to do it. "I saw a ghost once," she said, "and I've met somebody who's really good at telling fortunes. So I'm not sure I believe in witches but I'm not sure I don't." Then: "Was there a witch around here, like at Salem?"

"Why, yes, there was," said Mrs. Kellinger. Brightness trickled back into her face. "Would you like to hear the story? Once you know, you can make up your own mind about going any closer to the pines."

Jill gave Ariel a questioning look, and Ariel said, "Yes, please."

Mrs. Kellinger beamed at them again. "Why, then, come with me. Easier for all of us if we sit down." She turned and led the way back to the cottage.

It was not far from the edge of the pines, a one-story place with unpruned rose bushes on either side of the door. In the windows were curtains printed with images of white geese with yellow beaks and feet, decked out improbably in blue gingham sun bonnets. The deep porch in front had wicker furniture on it, a chair and a sofa, both painted white, both with cheap cushions on the seats decorated with the same geese in the same bonnets. Olive waved them to the sofa and settled slowly into the chair.

"All of this was a long, long time ago," she said, "back in colonial times, when Norton Hill west of here was the edge of the wilderness and the only people who lived on the other side of it were the Indians. All this country was pine woods then. What's now Lafayette Road wasn't much more than a deer trail. Criswell was a little village in those days with a dozen families and a church, farther west than any other settlement in this area—it really was a frontier village. Nobody lived further out this way but an old woman named Hepzibah Rewell. She had a little hut by Hoban's Pond, which is right in among the pines here, and she was a witch."

She glanced up at Ariel then, as though to gauge her reaction. Ariel nodded, and the old woman went on. "I never did read much about those witches at Salem, so I don't know if they were the same kind of thing, but I grew up not far from here and of course I heard stories about old Goody Rewell. Everybody knew about her back when I was a girl. They say she learned some of her trade back in the West Country in England before she crossed the ocean, and some more of it from the Indians once she got here. They say she could see the future by watching the pine needles fall into the water of the pond. They say she could talk to dead people and find out secrets from them, she could put on curses and take them off again, and heaven help you if you got her riled up, because nothing would go the way you wanted ever again.

"The way I heard it, she was thin as an old heron and bent over like one, and she only had one eye because she'd traded the other one for the power to see spirits. People would come to her cabin from all around the countryside and pay her in food and clothing and anything else she wanted, and she'd look into the future for them or cast spells for them, or she'd send her familiar to do things for her. Her familiar was supposed to be a devil in the shape of a big black raven, who could talk like a person and would fly around and spy for her."

Ariel kept her reaction off her face with an effort. Mrs. Kellinger sipped tea and went on. "The story goes that when she got near the end of her life and took sick, she knew right away that it was her last illness, and she sent that raven of hers to go to Criswell and get someone to come help her. Most of the people there were too scared of her to come, but one farmer thought that charity ought to extend even to witches, so he hitched up his horses to his wagon and drove out here as fast as he could. He got here in good time, put her in the wagon, and brought her back to his house, where his wife took care of her for the last few days before she died.

"The farmer's name was Tibbetts, Josiah Tibbetts, and his wife was named Priscilla. They didn't have any children yet, but before she died old Hepzibah Rewell blessed them for taking such good care of her. She said that their affairs would prosper and so would their heirs, for they would have a child within the year, a beautiful girl with golden hair. The one thing she asked of them was that no one would disturb the hut where she'd lived or the woods around it. They promised, and then she up and died, and they made sure she had a proper burial.

"Well, then, everything happened exactly as she said. From that day on, no matter what Josiah Tibbetts turned his hand to, it prospered, and not a year after the old witch died, Priscilla gave birth to a golden-haired daughter. They named her Patience, because they'd waited so long for a child, and she grew up to be the loveliest young woman in this whole part of the country. I'm sure you can imagine that the young men came buzzing around her like bees by a rosebush! Of course it wasn't just that she was pretty, she was also her father's only heir, and by then he'd prospered mightily, so whoever married her was going to become a very wealthy man. So the young men came courting, some rich and some poor, and finally Miss Patience Tibbetts said yes to a handsome young man named Samuel Kellinger from the next village over. Yes, he was my late husband's eleven-times-great grandfather.

"Now Sam Kellinger wasn't just handsome, he was smart and ambitious. He was a farmer's son and meant to be a farmer himself, but he wanted to become wealthy and respected, to sit in the colonial assembly and hobnob with rich men from England. So he bought a great stretch of land out here and started clearing it and building a big house for himself and his wife. He had the good sense to listen when his father-in-law told him what Hepzibah Rewell had asked, and so he fenced off the whole tract of pine woods around her hut and let everyone in the county know that he would flog them with a whip, never mind the laws, if they so much as took a single branch of firewood out of that place.

"Now Sam and Patience Kellinger prospered the way her parents had, and she had eight children and didn't lose one of them, which was practically a miracle in those days, you know.

The Kellingers became one of the first families in the colony and kept that same place when the colony became a state, one Kellinger got elected to the Continental Congress and three more served in the governor's mansion. Years and years went by, and all the while the Witch's Wood, as everyone called it, was safe and sound behind its fence. Of course most people wouldn't have risked going in there even if Sam Kellinger hadn't said what he did, because folks were scared of witches in those days.

"But then old Morton Kellinger died. He was my late husband's grandfather, and instead of leaving the land to his oldest son the way all his ancestors had done, and giving the others money and sending them on their way, he divided the land between his three sons. I don't know why, I don't think anyone does. But his oldest son Jasper got the mansion and all the land around it, and the other two sons, Anthony and Osborne, they got their own shares of the acreage. Jasper was the one who inherited this part of the estate, though it was much bigger then, and there was the big house Sam Kellinger built, which was back toward Criswell a mile or so, though it's long gone.

"Jasper Kellinger." The old woman shook her head. "That's a name you won't hear anyone praise round here. He put his money into the stock market in the 1920s, and lost it all in 1929 when the market crashed. Instead of waiting for the Kellinger luck to take care of him, he started selling off his farmland to raise money, and that meant his income fell off. Finally, fool that he was, he decided that he was going to clear most of the Witch's Wood and put the land into crops. Oh, the area right around the hut, the area that's still all pine trees, he left that alone, but the wood used to go all the way past the house east of here, most of a mile toward Criswell, and another mile north of Lafayette Road. He had to bring in people from out of the area to do the cutting and clear the stumps, nobody local would take his money for that, but he got the ground cleared and plowed and planted. And the night after the plowing was finished, that very night, Sam Kellinger's big house burned to the ground and he and his whole family were burned to death inside it. Not one of them got out alive.

"And that wasn't the end of it, because all the good luck the Kellingers had before then turned into bad luck from then on. Anthony, the second son, had three sons of his own, and all three of them went into the military when the Second World War broke out and they all got killed in action, one on Guadalcanal and one on a beach in Normandy and one on Okinawa, and their mother died of a broken heart and their father drank himself to death. As for Osborne, the youngest son, he got what was left of the estate by then, but he had health problems and money problems and he ended up having to sell off most of it, until there was barely enough to divide between his sons. My late husband Glen got this half and his younger brother Bill got the eastern half, and neither one of them could do much more than scrape by.

"So that's the story of the witch of Criswell and what happened to the Kellingers. And that's why you shouldn't go into the wood, especially not anywhere near the part that's by the pond. Old Hepzibah Rewell may be dead but that doesn't slow a witch down very much, you know. Maybe when the very last Kellinger's gone for good, she'll be satisfied, but—" She made a little motion, palms up. "Nobody knows but her, and she's not talking." Turning to Jill: "That's why I got so scared when that plate jumped off my table, and when you told me about things falling off the walls. My husband said once that his father told him the same thing happened in Jasper Kellinger's house before the fire, while the men were clearing most of the Witch's Wood. I don't know of any reason the witch might be upset at any of us, unless she's vexed because somebody went into the wood, but it doesn't hurt to be careful, you know."

Ariel waited for a moment, thinking about what her grandfather had said about the witch, and then asked, "Is there anything people can do to get on her good side? Something you can give her, and she'll give you good luck?"

Mrs. Kellinger glanced up. "Now where did you get that notion?"

Ariel put on a smile she didn't feel. "I read about it in a book. I forget where it was, but people used to do that at a witch's grave."

"Why, then, maybe there is, but I've never heard about it. I don't know where old Josiah Tibbetts buried her when she died, for all of that. I don't know if anyone does."

"Thank you for telling me the story," Ariel said then. "That's really something, that there used to be a witch here. I never heard about anything like that where I grew up." Then, because the old woman was still giving her a worried look: "And I'll stay away from the woodlot."

Mrs. Kellinger's face relaxed visibly, and she beamed at them both. "Thank you, dear. I don't know if there's anything to worry about, really, but I wouldn't want anyone to find out the hard way. And with those pictures falling and all—" She shuddered visibly.

Jill and Ariel thanked her and said their goodbyes, and went back across the barnyard, while Olive went inside her cottage. The afternoon had gotten even more sultry and still. Off in the distance, the porch of the brown house was empty at first, but then the woman in the blue sun dress came out again and stood there, as though watching them. Ariel considered saying something to Jill, but just then an ugly croaking call sounded from high up in one of the nearby pines. Ariel glanced up and spotted the big raven perched there, as though looking down at them. She glanced at Jill, and was met by an uneasy look.

## CHAPTER 7

# A WISH COMES TRUE

Ariel brought the Buick to a halt where Lafayette Road ended and the Old Federal Pike stretched away to both sides. "So that's everything she told me," she said. "Do you think maybe the witch is behind the stuff that happened to Jill and Ben?"

"Possibly," said Dr. Moravec.

She gave him a dubious glance, but his face was as unreadable as always. Just then the traffic opened up, and she took the turn and started east toward Adocentyn.

"You're not going to guess," she said then.

"I never guess," the old man replied at once. "It is a shocking habit, destructive to the logical faculty."

She looked at him again, saw the raised eyebrow. "You got that from Sherlock Holmes."

"Good. Yes, it's from *The Sign of the Four*. You're a fan of mysteries?"

"Kind of. I read all the Nancy Drew books when I was in grade school, and then started on some other mystery stories once I got into middle school. Holmes and Lord Peter Wimsey especially. They're really good."

"Good," said Dr. Moravec. "Tell me this. How would Holmes or Wimsey solve this little mystery of ours?"

She thought about that while a few blocks rolled past and Adocentyn's skyscrapers came closer. "Holmes would notice all kinds of little things," she said then, "footprints and ciga- rette ashes and who had what kind of mud on their boots, and he'd know right away who did it. Wimsey would notice lots of things, too, but mostly he'd get people talking, and listen to what they said. He'd put things together one clue at a time and finally announce who did it after he got the last clue he needed."

"Even better." He shook his head. "I'm sorry to say I wasn't able to get a clear sense of who might be behind this, so the methods of Holmes and Wimsey will be needed." After another moment: "Perhaps you can tell me what you noticed at Mrs. Kellinger's farm."

A block of strip malls went past before she answered. "I don't think Jill and Ben are faking it. They acted like they're really scared."

"Did you think they might be faking?"

Ariel shrugged. "That happens a lot in books." She changed lanes. "I'm pretty sure they're right and there's no other way into the basement. Even if there was a hidden tunnel or some- thing, there's so much junk piled up around the walls that you couldn't get past it."

Dr. Moravec nodded, said nothing.

"That matters because if someone gets into the basement, either it's a ghost or someone has a spare key. Well, two spare keys."

"One," the old man said. "From the condition of the lock on the front door, they leave the doors unlocked. Most people in farm country still do that."

She nodded, drove on.

"Jill took you to see the horses," Dr. Moravec said then. "And the barn. Did you notice anything out of the ordinary there?"

Moments passed while she considered that. "I don't know a lot about barns," she said. "I've never been in one before, except for the horse barns in summer camp, and those aren't the same. But I didn't see anything that seemed weird to me. I don't think it's been used for anything but horses for a long time. There are a couple of tractors there, but they're pretty rusty, and the other farm equipment was in the same kind of shape." She paused, then: "I read some books where animals got really freaky around ghosts and things like that. Does that happen with—with the stuff that witches do?"

"With magic? It can," said the old man. "It depends on the magic. Some magic is in harmony with the cosmos, and some is not. Animals are sensitive to that. So are people, if they don't blind themselves to it. A working that's in harmony with the cosmos spreads the harmony all around it, and animals can feel that. A friend of mine, another trustee of the Heydonian, has six cats, and when she gets ready to perform a ritual they all insist on being let into the room so they can sit in the corners and watch."

Ariel laughed. "That's the bee's knees."

"But yes, it works the other way around. The kind of magic that's out of harmony with the cosmos, animals dislike that, and let you know about it." He paused. "And outside, in the farmyard? Did you notice anything else?"

"There's a woman in the brown house further west," said Ariel. "It looked like she was watching me and Jill when we were out back behind the barn. I can't be sure of it, but both times we were out there she came out on the porch and she was facing toward us."

"From the Northams' house."

"Yeah. And there was a raven." She slowed as the traffic thickened. "A really big one. It was on the roof watching when we got there, and I saw it again when Jill and I left Mrs. Kellinger's cottage. Mrs. Kellinger said the witch had a raven for a familiar—and Aunt Clarice saw a raven when she read the tea leaves for me."

"I saw it when we arrived," said Dr. Moravec.

"Do witches really have familiars like that? I thought that was just in stories."

"You're thinking," he said, "of the Bertie Scrubb novels."

Ariel sent a doubtful glance his way, partly because she was startled that he'd so much as heard of that series of children's novels, popular though they were, and partly because he'd said the last three words as though they tasted bad. "Well, partly," she admitted.

"I hope they're not favorites of yours."

"No, not at all." Memories of a vanished enthusiasm challenged that utterance, and she revised it: "Well, okay, I thought the first one was the cat's meow when I first read it, but I was eleven then. When I took the third one back to the library I was so tired of the whole thing that I went straight to the fiction shelves and checked out the first book I saw up on top, where the librarians put things they want you to look at. It was *The Great Gatsby*, and—" She shrugged. "I don't even know how many Bertie Scrubb books there are now."

"Thirteen, I'm sorry to say," said Dr. Moravec. In a weary tone: "Ever since the first one came out, the Heydonian has been fielding letters from teenagers who insist they've seen the Magic Sign and want to tell us that they're the next Bertie Scrubb. The secretaries send them a form letter, but it doesn't always work. We've had some show up and throw tantrums because Mabel Figworthy won't come out on demand and teach them."

"Oh, really," said Ariel; that was Miss Figworthy's invariable comment in the novels. Dr. Moravec gave her an unsanitary look, and she stifled a grin and said, "There isn't really a Magic Sign, is there? Or anything like that?"

"No." The old man shook his head. "One of the most annoying things about those books is that they treat magic as something that only special people can learn."

Startled, Ariel considered that. "So can anybody learn magic?"

"Of course. Anyone who's willing to study the classic texts, take up the necessary exercises and meditations, and work like a dog."

"Aunt Clarice said you have to be gifted for the work," she ventured.

Unexpectedly, he allowed a slight smile. "I'm sure she did. She and I have our disagreements, and that's one of them." He looked out the window again. "May I ask a favor of you? Please forget everything you read about magic in those dreadful books. What I study and the Heydonian teaches has nothing to do with talking wallabies or evil hedgehogs, and nobody, no matter what sign they've seen, can throw thunderbolts from their fingertips. Yes, some witches have familiar spirits who take animal forms, but that's the only resemblance."

After a moment, when he'd said nothing more, Ariel sent a look his way. He was observing the traffic as though nothing mattered in the world. Another block, and Old Federal Pike dissolved into a tangle of streets going in three different directions. Ariel was sure she was lost until the big central dome of the Heydonian, glimpsed between two brick buildings of Victorian vintage, gave her her bearings. From there, with only a little help from her grandfather, she found her way back to the tall green house on Lyon Avenue promptly enough.

Once they got home, Dr. Moravec spent the rest of the afternoon in his study, poring over big leather-bound tomes and taking notes in a battered spiral notebook. At dinner he was distracted, his thoughts obviously elsewhere, and Ariel didn't try to lead him into conversation. Afterwards, she settled in the parlor and he went back to his study. As the dim murmur of traffic outside faded, the scratching of his pen became audible in the hush.

Lacking anything better to do, Ariel brooded over what she'd seen at the farm, then got out her e-reader and went searching through the reams of old books she'd downloaded for the summer. Luck was with her—she'd provided herself with two collections of Sherlock Holmes stories and all the Lord Peter Wimsey novels. A moment passed before she decided between them and spent a couple of hours following the exploits of Arthur Conan Doyle's famous sleuth, trying to imagine him pacing around the Kellinger farmyard, his keen eyes interpreting every faint mark in the dust around the farmyard, his icy intellect fitting every clue into its inevitable place.

That stirred restless thoughts, and those still waited for her when she got up the next morning. After breakfast her grandfather set off for the Heydonian Institution, where he had a meeting. Ariel weighed the options and went to the Culpeper Hill public library. She had to choke back a laugh when she passed the new book shelf, for right there in the middle of the shelf of new fiction for kids was *The Amazing Voyage of Bertie Scrubb.* "Number thirteen in the bestselling series!" the cover yelled in big yellow letters. She went on past it without a second glance, though. She had more important things on her mind.

She'd been a book geek since earliest childhood and that gave her certain advantages. It took next to no time for her to chase down the shelves where books on local history drowsed the morning away, and only a little more to find the section on folklore. Two books on witch legends and three volumes on the history of the part of the state that included Criswell went with her to a table by one of the big arched windows, and she went to work on them with an enthusiasm she'd rarely put into her high school work.

One of the books on witches had a story about a witch in France who'd had a raven familiar and another one who kept herself young and pretty for a century by taking other people's life force from them. It spoke more generally about the different kinds of witches, those who healed and those who harmed and those who did both, those who practiced witchcraft for other people like Hepzibah Rewell, and those who cast spells only for themselves. The other book talked of a witch's grave in Cornwall where a thorn tree grew, and the local people tied little lengths of ribbon to the branches and made wishes there, hoping the witch would help them: white ribbon to heal and bless, red to seek revenge against an enemy. Ariel noted the details down in a text file on her phone. They were the only clues she found that seemed to have any bearing on the Kellinger farm, though the books gave her plenty to think about in another way.

Witches weren't something she'd ever thought to deal with in the real world. A wicked witch named Maledicta Gabble featured in the Bertie Scrubb novels as one of the sidekicks of Lord Roderick Dudgeon, the villain of the series. She'd known a couple of girls in high school who said they were witches, for that matter, though that just meant that they were into Wicca and liked to swish around in gauzy black clothing. Old Hepzibah Rewell was something different, Ariel felt sure of that, and so was Aunt Clarice Jackson. The two books on witches showed her that for centuries on centuries, people had known about witches like those two, feared them, and gone to them for any number of purposes, good or bad.

The books on local history had more to say about the case itself, for the Kellingers had been just as important in the affairs of the colony as Olive had said, and the story of the witch of Criswell and the blessing she'd given the heirs of Josiah and Priscilla Tibbetts had a prominent place in local folklore as a result. She couldn't find much about the Kellingers after the 1850s, however, and none of the books mentioned the Witch's Wood or the promise the Tibbetts had made to keep it unchanged. A search through the indexes turned up one more detail: a brief reference to the fire that had destroyed the old Kellinger mansion in 1938 and the deaths of the entire family. She noted that down, too.

Once she'd finished going through the books, she sat back and stared at nothing in particular for a long while. It might be the ghost of Hepzibah Rewell, she thought, who was behind the trouble Jill and Ben were having. It might be some other ghost or spirit. Or it might be someone living: that was what her grandfather had said. If it was the witch's ghost, maybe it was upset because someone went into the woods, or maybe there was some other reason. If it was a different spirit, it would have some reason to make trouble—or would it? It occurred to her that she ought to ask her grandfather why spirits did things.

But if it was a living person …

Bitter rivalries and smoldering hatreds she'd watched play out at high school came to mind, and so did her grandfather's comments about curses on cows and feuds passed down through the generations. She could easily imagine some tangled resentment driving one of the other families in the area to put a curse on the Kellinger farm, maybe intending to cost Olive Kellinger a tenant, maybe with some other unpleasant goal in mind. Maybe, she thought, maybe that's the key. Find out which of the neighbors are angry at Mrs. Kellinger, or have a grudge against the Kellinger family that's been carried over from some earlier time, and that might point to the one who's casting the spell.

That was when reality intruded. She'd been lucky to get the chance to go out to the farm once, but she guessed Dr. Moravec wouldn't keep taking her along once he got to work on the investigation. Maybe there would be another chance after that, but maybe there wouldn't, and in eight weeks, no matter what happened, she'd be boarding the train to Summerfield and a life that seemed even more cramped and dismal than ever.

Scowling, she took the books back to their places, and in a sudden fit of defiance went looking for a book on how real private investigators solved cases. That took a few minutes to hunt down, but she finally spotted a thick well-illustrated book on the subject, checked it out, and left the library for her grandfather's house, resolving to read it that very day.

She was two chapters into it when Dr. Moravec got back from his meeting. After a brief distracted greeting that left

Ariel wondering if he'd actually noticed her existence, he buried himself in his study again with a big stack of astrological charts. She glanced after him and plunged back into the details of chasing down details about people who had something to hide. That book kept her busy until dinner, and afterwards she dove into a Lord Peter Wimsey mystery novel and spent the next few hours pleasantly enough, watching over the shoulder of Dorothy Sayers's amateur detective as he went undercover at an advertising agency.

As she finished the novel, reality intruded again. Lord Peter Wimsey could take as much time as he wanted to chase down a murderer and foil a sinister drug ring, but untitled eighteen-year-old Ariel Moravec didn't have that option. She went up to her bedroom in a foul mood, and even with Nicodemus's familiar presence, it took a long time for her to get to sleep.

The next morning's text from her mother didn't help. It didn't start with a good morning or even Ariel's name, it just launched straight into a tirade: I LITERALLY BURST INTO TEARS ON THE RUTGERS CAMPUS YESTERDAY AFTERNOON WHEN I THOUGHT OF ALL THE OPPORTUNITIES YOU THREW AWAY, and went on in the same vein for three and a half more screens before finishing up with a series of angry questions about Ariel's future that Ariel couldn't yet answer and didn't want to try.

Ariel was in tears, too, by the time she finished reading the whole thing, but they were tears of anger. She thought again of snapping the phone in half and throwing it away, but she knew better than to do it. Instead, she started writing a furious response, then caught herself and deleted it. The phone went back on the vanity while she showered and dressed. Once that was done, two taps on the screen deleted the text from her mother before she could succumb to the temptation to read it again. A quick flurry of thumb strokes wrote an answer: MOM THX FOR YOUR CONCERN WE CAN TALK ABOUT IT LATER OK? A.

One more jab with a thumb sent the text on its way. She didn't have to guess how her mother would take the response, so she put the phone on mute, set it back on the vanity, and glared at it. My leash, she thought, mocking herself. With that in her mind she turned and went downstairs trying to think of some way she could manage to enjoy the day anyway.

Dr. Moravec forestalled her by coming out of his study as she got to the bottom of the stairs. "Good morning, Ariel. I just fielded a call from our clients and I'd like to talk to you for a few moments, if you don't mind."

"Sure," said Ariel, grinning despite herself at the words "our clients." She followed her grandfather into the parlor and settled in what had become her usual place on one side of the sofa, where the crocodile's cold bright gaze could cheer her. "So what's the news?"

Dr. Moravec settled into his armchair. "Someone tried to get into the cellar at the Kellinger house last night," he said. "Ben had the great good sense to put a little piece of tape on the door to the broom closet where it wouldn't be noticed, and it was broken this morning. The cellar door was still locked, he had tape on it as well, and the talismans I put in the cellar hadn't been touched. It looks as though someone expected to find the key in its usual place."

"So it really is someone living," Ariel said.

"That's certainly how it looks. Jill and Ben wanted to know if I could come out there today. Unfortunately there are some issues before the board today, and I can't be spared. So I wonder if you would be willing to spend a few days out at the Kellinger farm, to keep an eye on things and call me at once if you notice anything out of the ordinary." An eyebrow went up. "If it's any incentive, Jill mentioned something or other about riding horses."

Ariel realized after a moment that her mouth was open, and shut it. Sometimes, she thought, sometimes wishes really do come true. "Duck soup," she said, and then hoped he realized the words meant of course she could. "And I just read a book from the library on how private investigators do things, so I might even be able to help out a little. Figuring out what's going on, I mean."

"Did you? Good." He reached into a pocket, brought out a leather shape like a flat wallet, and held it out to her. She reached for it and opened it. On one half of the inside was a well-worn silver badge with the words PRIVATE INVESTIGATOR on it, and on the other a state card with his name and photo and various other details, including those same two words.

Her mouth fell open again, though she caught the movement this time and stopped it halfway. "You're a private eye? Seriously? That's—" She sorted hurriedly through her stock of Jazz Age slang to find something enthusiastic enough. "Absolute *berries*."

He shrugged, deflecting the compliment. "The state laws don't look fondly on ordinary citizens poking about in each other's affairs. So the license is helpful, and it covers any assistants I might happen to have."

Ariel handed back the badge wallet, and then let herself sink back into the sofa. "Thank you. Seriously, thank you."

"Of course. Now." He raised a finger. "Your job is to watch, take notes, ask questions if you have any, and keep me informed of whatever you observe and whatever you find out. If you find anything that looks as though it has to do with magic, mail it to me here as quickly as you can—I'll give you some envelopes. If anything else out of the ordinary happens, don't get involved unless you have no other options, and call me at once no matter what the time, day or night. Understood?"

"Yeah." Grinning again: "You're the shamus, I'm just the girl Friday."

Dr. Moravec nodded. "Good. In that case, you might want to pack and get some breakfast while I give our clients a call."

## CHAPTER 8

# THE ROWAN GROVE

The blue Nissan hybrid lurched to a halt in front of the Kellinger farmhouse. Ariel climbed out, extracted her suitcase from the back seat, and stood waiting. Jill, moving at a more leisurely pace, got out from behind the driver's seat, sent a smile Ariel's way, and led her into the house. "We told Olive that Cousin Ariel was going to be staying with us for a few days," she said once the door was closed. "Ben and I thought the fewer people know that you work for an investigator, the better."

Ariel thanked her, waited by the stair while she ducked into the parlor to let Ben know they were back, and then followed her upstairs to a pleasant little bedroom. The one window had a good view of the farmyard, from the near end of the barn to Mrs. Kellinger's cottage up against the woodlot. When Ariel stood close to the window and looked off to the left she could see the Northams' house. No one was on the porch just then.

She turned, said to Jill, "Thank you. This is great."

"You're welcome. Let's see—the blue towel and washcloth in the bath are for you, and there should be plenty of room for your makeup in the cabinet."

"I don't have any makeup," Ariel said. With a shrug: "I can't wear it. Every brand I ever tried makes me break out."

Jill gave her an uncertain look, but nodded and went on. "If you need anything else, let me know. What's on your to-do list?"

"I'm supposed to keep an eye on things," said Ariel, "take notes, ask questions, and call Dr. Moravec the minute anything happens. I should ask you and Ben about what happened with the broom closet overnight, but that's the only thing in the list right away."

Jill nodded. "This is about the time I usually give the horses some exercise by taking them out for a gallop. It shouldn't take too long for Ben and me to fill you in about what happened. We made sure not to touch anything, if that helps. After that, if you think you can make room for some time in the saddle, I'm sure Corazon would love to oblige. Have you ridden before?"

For once, Ariel had reason to bless the summer camps where she'd spent so many bored and lonely weeks in childhood. "Yeah. Um, it's been a few years."

Jill's smile dismissed that. "I'm sure you'll do fine."

"Thank you," said Ariel. "And yes, please, I'd love to go riding."

"I once met a girl who didn't like horses," said Jill as they went back down the stairs. "Just once. But you and Corazon seemed to get along pretty well. Besides, it'll give you the chance to see the property and a little of the area around it."

"I was thinking of that," Ariel said, not entirely truthfully.

It didn't take long for her to note down everything Ben and Jill had to say about the broom closet and the attempt to get into the cellar. Both of them had slept soundly, and no noise from downstairs had disturbed them. The only sign that something was amiss was the broken piece of tape on the closet door. Ariel snapped a photo of that on her phone and sent it to her grandfather along with the text file she'd filled with what they'd told her, then glanced around the kitchen. She found herself wishing that she'd asked Dr. Moravec for a fingerprint kit, if he had one. The book on private investigation went on in detail about dusting surfaces for fingerprints, and it annoyed Ariel to think that the solution to the mystery might be right there on the bright brass handle of the kitchen closet.

A sudden idea seized her. She knelt, got her face close to the knob, and breathed onto it with the kind of slow soft breath that fogs glass. It fogged the handle, too, and she could see the faint marks of fingers on it, but no fingerprints at all. One of the finger marks had what looked like the trace of a wrinkle on it. By then the clouding had faded, and she breathed on the knob again and got two pictures with her smartphone.

She stood up to find Ben and Jill staring at her. "I didn't even think of that," Ben said. "What did you find?"

Ariel had to fight to keep a grin off her face. "When was the last time somebody cleaned the closet doorknob?"

"Yesterday afternoon," said Jill. "I'm kind of fussy about that. My shrink back in California thinks I have borderline OCD."

"Then whoever came in had rubber gloves on. They didn't leave any prints."

Ben and Jill glanced at each other, a sudden quick look Ariel didn't know how to read. She used the silence to send those photos to her grandfather, too, then pocketed the phone, asked about whether the outside doors were ever locked, and got the answer she expected: "No, never," said Ben. "We were hoping to get away from that when we left California, and everyone we talked to told us that nobody locks their doors out here."

She filed that away for future reference, went back upstairs to change into jeans and a plain blouse, and five minutes later was following Jill into the barn. "No, Ben doesn't ride," she was saying. "He grew up in the middle of Oakland and horses were something he saw in old cowboy movies. He doesn't get along well with animals." She glanced up. "Oh, hi, Ricky. Everything's okay with the horses?"

It took Ariel a moment to spot the stocky shape halfway across the barn: a young woman with a square muscular build and brown hair cut in an unflattering style, dressed in worn jeans and a blue flannel shirt. "Yeah," Ricky said in a flat voice. "They're fine."

"Good. This is my cousin Ariel, who's staying with us for a couple of days. She'll be riding Corazon today."

Ricky made a vague noise in her throat and turned away toward the horses before Ariel could greet her or do anything else. Jill went the same way, and Ariel followed her. By the time she and Jill reached the two occupied stalls Ricky was back with a saddle on one shoulder and the rest of the tackle for one horse in the other hand. "I can saddle her if you want," the girl said, looking away.

By then Ariel had begun to get her measure. "Please. You know more about it than I do."

That earned her a little uncertain glance and something that might have been the first ghost of a smile. She got out of the way as Ricky got the halter on Corazon's head with a minimum of fuss, led the mare out of the stall, threw open the barn's back doors and got to work with the saddle. Meanwhile Jill fetched the bigger saddle Stormalong needed and started on the same process. Ariel stood over to one side and watched until Ricky was finished and turned toward her, the reins in one hand.

"Thanks," Ariel said, taking the reins only when Ricky offered them, and making sure not to try to meet the girl's eyes. "You're good at that."

Ricky mumbled something and looked away, but something a little closer to a smile tensed one side of her face. She waited while Ariel got one foot up into the near stirrup and swung a little awkwardly into the saddle, then patted Corazon gently on the shoulder and backed away. The mare walked sedately out into the barnyard, stopped, and swung her head around to look at Ariel, as though to say, well, what now?

Ariel spent a moment frantically trying to remember everything she'd learned about horseback riding. By the time she'd finished Jill and Stormalong were out of the barn and coming up to join them. Corazon, apparently deciding that the matter was settled, fell in alongside the gelding, and the two horses went placidly through the open gate into the pasture while Jill sat comfortably and Ariel tried to look less clumsy than she felt.

"Don't mind Ricky," Jill said once they'd gone into the pasture and the barn was out of earshot. "She's a lot better with horses than she is with people."

"She's autistic, isn't she?" said Ariel.

That earned her a startled look. "Yes. Is it that obvious?"

"I knew a couple of autistic girls in high school." Ariel shrugged. "Us geeks and losers had to stick together."

Another look, hard to read. "I'm going to guess that you were one of the geeks."

"Depends on who you ask," said Ariel.

They rode on a little while in silence, going north across the pasture. Off to the left, past a white fence and a quarter mile of field with young corn on it, the Northams' house loomed up against the green uneven shapes of the hills, and there was June Northam, standing on the porch watching them go. To the right, the woodlot ran the full length of the pasture, thick with old dark pines and shadows.

"This whole business with the witch, if that's what it is," Jill said then. With a nervous laugh: "Like something out of those kids' novels."

"Bertie Scrubb," Ariel ventured.

"Yes. Except it's not so fun if you're in the middle of it. I sometimes wonder if everyone around here grows up with this kind of thing."

"Tell me about the neighbors," Ariel said. "Please. What are they like?"

"We don't actually see much of them," Jill admitted. "The Northams are your basic hardworking farm folks. He's got his tractor out just about every day, and she's always at home, though she comes out on the porch a lot. They've got their own farm and they also rent most of Olive's acreage, so there's a lot to do. Bill and Dot Kellinger I've seen a couple of times. I don't think they're doing well at all, but we've never said anything but 'Hi, how are you?' Oscar Bremberg I've talked to just once, and it wasn't a good experience."

Ariel gave her an uncertain glance, and Jill went on. "I was walking to Criswell—it's not far, and I do that pretty often to stretch my legs and get my mind clear for painting. I'd just left the property. He was in his driveway, and he had one of his antique cars out—he's got two of them, I don't know what kind they are. But he was doing some kind of repair, and then he saw me and walked over to the road, so I slowed down and crossed halfway. I was about to say hi when he said, 'You're renting from the Kellinger woman.' I said yes, my husband and I are, and he gave me this unpleasant look and said, 'You won't stay long. Better pack your bags.' Then he turned his back on me and went back to the car he was working on. I didn't say anything, I just kept on walking."

Ariel thought about that. After a moment, she asked, "Was this before or after you started having the trouble?"

Jill gave her another startled look. "Before," she said. "In fact, it was that night or the night after, I forget which one, that Ben and I first heard the footsteps. Do you think—" She let the rest of the question go unasked.

Ariel shrugged. "I don't know. I'll make sure to tell Dr. Moravec, though."

As the end of the pasture came close, Ariel wondered for a moment where they would go next, then spotted the gate over on the right, where the woodlot ended. A dirt road beyond it headed off toward Criswell. The horses didn't have to wonder, and angled across the pasture to the gate. Corazon slowed and stopped. Stormalong went right up to the gate and stood patiently while Jill swung down and got the gate open. "Go on through," she said to Ariel; Corazon, without waiting for any further urging, walked onto the road and then waited while

Jill led the gelding through the gate, closed it behind them, and mounted again.

"This is where I usually let them gallop," Jill said then. "You can keep a slower pace if you like, though."

"I'll be fine," Ariel said, and tried to make herself believe it.

Jill grinned and snapped the reins, and Stormalong broke into a gallop toward Criswell. Corazon glanced back at Ariel, who made sure of her seat and then snapped the reins the same way. The mare's expression said, "Sure, if you want" as clearly as words could have done, and she started after the gelding at a slightly more demure gallop.

The dirt road went along the north side of the woodlot and then out past it, cutting between sagging fences and green cornfields on both sides. Ariel let Corazon run and put all her attention into keeping her seat and moving along with the mare, as she'd been taught in summer camp. Five minutes or so of exhilaration edged with stark terror ended as Ariel and Corazon both caught sight of Jill and Stormalong waiting for them up ahead. The mare slowed smoothly and came to a halt next to the gelding. Only then did Ariel notice, north of the road, a break in the monotony of the cornfields: old squared stones among unmown grass and weeds, with a scattering of low bushy trees she didn't recognize growing off past them.

"Remember Olive's story about the Kellinger mansion?" Jill said, gesturing at the stones. "The one that burned down? This is where it was and the stones are what's left of it. There's a photo of it in the Criswell post office."

Ariel pondered the scene, tried to make sense of the scattered stones, and wondered if the sense of desolation she felt was just an echo of Mrs. Kellinger's story. The breeze made low hissing sounds in among the branches of the trees.

"It used to be quite a place," Jill went on. "The trees over past it are rowans, from England—the clerk at the general store told me that one of the Kellingers had an English wife and planted one to please her, and all those are descended from it."

She motioned down the road. "We can't go much further that way. The old Criswell cemetery's about half a mile on, and the horses won't go past that no matter what. There are some other routes, but you said you haven't ridden in a while and I'm going to guess that you're already feeling it."

She was right, of course. Ariel looked away and said, "Well, kind of."

Jill grinned. "Back home, then. If you're up for it we can do this again tomorrow."

Ariel didn't argue, and a moment later the two horses were walking at a sedate pace side by side up the dirt road. "Do you know anything about—" Ariel fumbled briefly for words. "Grudges and things like that between Olive and the neighbors, or anyone else nearby?"

That got her a long considering look from Jill. "There's some kind of bad blood between Olive and the other Kellingers, Bill and Dot. I don't know what it is. Olive just looks sad and shakes her head whenever anything about it comes up. Oscar Bremberg, the way he talked to me that one time, it wouldn't surprise me if he had some kind of problem with Olive."

"The Northams?"

"Good question. They rent from Olive, of course, and Fred is always polite when he comes over, but he doesn't come often and he doesn't spend a minute longer than he has to. I've never talked to his wife."

"Is she the one that was on the porch the last time I was here?"

"That's her. I don't know if she's just snoopy or what, but she watches us a lot."

Ariel pondered that as the horses ambled back along the dirt road. Off to the left, above the cornstalks, she could see the rundown blue barn Bill and Dot Kellinger owned, and the much-patched roof of their house to one side of it. To the right, fields stretched away into the distance over long low folds of countryside. A hawk traced mathematical circles against the sky, then veered off in another direction and went out of sight. Not long after it was gone, another bird came flying up from somewhere behind them, beating the air with heavy wing strokes: a big raven. It flew past them, following the road, and then turned in a graceless arc and vanished in among the pines of the woodlot.

Ten minutes and a little desultory talk brought them back to the pasture gate, and from there to the barn. Ricky had apparently finished her chores and gone home, and so Ariel helped with the process of getting the horses unsaddled, curried, brushed, and back in their stalls with hay and water. By the time that was finished, and the saddles and tack were back in their places on the wall of the barn, every muscle from her waist to her knees was yelling at her in a different shrill voice. It took some effort not to hobble as she followed Jill from the barn to the house, though she did her best, and thanked Jill profusely for the chance to go riding. Jill laughed and thanked her for giving Corazon a little exercise.

By the time they got to the kitchen door, the first thought in Ariel's mind was a shower, followed by clothes a little less fragrant with horse sweat and an hour or so not using her legs much. She came through the door to find Ben putting down the kitchen phone.

"Your timing's good," he said to both of them. "That was Dot Kellinger. She says they've got a barn door that's coming loose and the pins for that style of hinge aren't made any more. She wants to know if she could come over and see if there's one in the collection of spare parts in Glen Kellinger's workshop."

It took Ariel an instant to catch the implication. "In the cellar."

"Bingo. She'll be here in half an hour. Maybe it's a coincidence, but—" He shrugged. "Dr. Moravec said somebody might try to get down there. I guess he was right."

## CHAPTER 9

# A GLITTER IN THE DARKNESS

Twenty minutes later Ariel finished toweling herself off, gave her disheveled hair a bleak look, and skinned into underwear, tee shirt, and boy shorts. She'd called her grandfather while Jill showered, and had to leave a message—he was still meeting with the board of trustees, she guessed. That stirred cold scared feelings down in her belly, but she faced those down. *Don't get involved unless you have no other options*: that was what he'd said, but since she'd called him and hadn't gotten an answer, she couldn't think of any other options. She was in the middle of things, she told herself, and she'd just have to deal.

She got socks and shoes on, spent a minute she probably couldn't spare trying to get her hair to behave itself, and then pocketed her phone and headed down the stairs to the parlor. Ben was sitting on the couch reading a paperback with a gaudy cover. He glanced up at her as she came in, nodded, went back to his book. Ariel found a chair, checked her phone again—nothing from her grandfather yet, the screen told her—and tucked it back into the right hand pocket of her shorts, then settled down to wait.

A few minutes passed before a tentative knocking sounded on the front door. As they'd arranged, Ariel got up and went to open it. Outside on the porch was a thin hard-faced woman in a faded yellow dress. Her graying hair was pulled back hard in a braid, and she had a white vinyl purse clutched in both hands. She gave Ariel a wary look through cheap plastic-rimmed glasses.

"Oh, hi," said Ariel, before the woman could respond. "You must be Dot Kellinger. I'm Jill Callahan's cousin Ariel. Ben's waiting to let you into the cellar. Come on in."

"Pleased to meet you," said the woman, after a frozen moment. "Yes, that's me. Thank you." She came inside, waited while Ariel closed the door, and then followed her into the parlor. Ben got to his feet to greet her and shake her hand. Jill was nowhere in sight; she was waiting in her studio with her phone in her hand, just in case.

"Now you wanted something from the cellar, right?" Ben said then. "Sure thing. I haven't spent much time down there but I know there's plenty of spare parts and stuff." He led the way into the kitchen, got the key out of his pocket and unlocked the door on the far side of the refrigerator. "Ariel, can you go with her? Thanks."

Ariel smiled and nodded, as though they hadn't planned the whole thing out in advance. She waved Dot Kellinger ahead, waited while the older woman went through the door and turned on the lights, then followed her down the stairs into the clutter and long shadows of the cellar.

The next stage was the trickiest part. Ariel hung back at the foot of the stairs until she knew for certain that Dot was going to the workbench, then followed slowly, as though bored, keeping the woman in sight the whole time. It didn't surprise her at all when Dot went straight for the end of the workbench where Dr. Moravec had hidden one of the protective talismans. She let herself drift to the other end of the workbench and faced away.

After a brief search and a few minutes of planning, Ben had extracted one of the discarded full-length mirrors from the basement junk, and propped it up against a steamer trunk so that the largest of its remaining silvered patches gave a perfect view of the workbench if you stood in just the right place. Ariel found the right place, waited, and watched. She turned so that her right side was hidden from Dot, then extracted her phone from her pocket as surreptitiously as she could. She woke it and pressed one of the buttons on the screen with her thumb, keeping it out of sight the whole time.

Dot searched through a couple of jars of assorted spare parts, making little sidelong glances at Ariel now and then. Had she noticed the mirror, or the phone? It didn't look that way, Ariel thought. Maybe she really is here for a hinge pin—

At that moment, with one more sidelong look, Dot crouched down suddenly and reached under the workbench. Ariel turned just as quickly and brought up the phone. The flash of the camera cast sudden hard shadows against the walls. Dot let out a frightened cry and jerked back. The flash went off again as Ariel snapped another photo, and something fell from Dot's hand onto the stone floor, where it hit with a chime like metal. A third flash caught the thing clearly, but it was round and golden, not one of the square pieces of gray metal Dr. Moravek had hidden.

"Okay," said Ben, from the foot of the stairs. Ariel jumped. She hadn't heard even the faintest sound as he'd come down into the cellar. "Mrs. Kellinger, why don't you take a couple of steps back from that and keep your hands where I can see them."

The harsh light from the bare bulbs overhead made Dot's face look the color of bleached bone. She looked from Ben to Ariel and back again, pressed her lips together, then backed away from the workbench and forced out in a shaking voice, "It—it's not what it looks like—"

"Maybe not, but—" Ben started to say, as he crossed the room, and then stopped. He was staring at the thing that had fallen from Dot's hand. Ariel looked that way, and stared, too. It was a gold coin, a big one, and it looked antique.

Ben crossed the cellar, stepped over to the coin and scooped it up. It glinted in his hand as he turned it one way, the other. He faced Dot. "Mrs. Kellinger, I think we all need to go upstairs, and then you're going to tell Jill and Ariel and me what all this is about. I don't want to call the county sheriff or anyone else unless I have to."

Dot gave a sudden start when he mentioned the sheriff, then ducked her head. Once he finished talking, she started for the stair.

Once they were back up the stairs and the cellar door was locked again, Ben led her into the parlor while Ariel went ahead and fetched Jill with a quick gesture. "Have a seat," Ben said to all of them, and waited until Dot was huddled in one of the chairs before he sat down on the sofa, where Jill joined him. Then he handed the gold coin to Jill, who sucked in a sudden hard breath when she looked at it.

"I'll point out the obvious," said Ben. "That's not a hinge pin. Mrs. Kellinger, you're going to have to tell us why it was there, and why you knew it was there."

Dot shrank down into her chair and said nothing. Ben waited for a while, and then said, "In that case I'm going to have to call the sheriff's office."

"No!" The word burst out of her in a little frightened squeak. "It's nothing the sheriff has any business knowing about."

"Convince me," said Ben.

She hunched her shoulders and said, "It should have been ours. The old man left a share to each of his sons and told my Bill where to find his, but Glen, that's his brother who's gone now, said there wasn't a will and there wasn't any left, Osborne Kellinger handed it all over back in '33 when Roosevelt took everyone's gold."

Ben waited for a moment, then said, "And you left it there until now?"

"I only took one when we didn't have any other choice," said Dot. "Only when Bill and I would have lost the farm otherwise, and the good Lord knows what would have become of us then. But just this month the cows started giving milk like they're supposed to, and we've got to get the spare milking machine fixed, and this was the last of old Mr. Morton's gold, and I thought—I thought—" She started crying.

After a frozen moment, Jill got up, found a box of tissues and handed it to Dot, who gave her a look half grateful and half wary, and pulled out a tissue to dab her face. Once she'd finished, Ben said, "And that's why you tried to get into the cellar last night."

If she was faking her response, Ariel thought, she was good at it. She gave Ben a horrified look and said, "Last night? Good Lord, no. I don't go out at night, and I don't care what you think, I'm not a thief. I did what I always do. I called you the way I called the other people who rented here and asked for something from the cellar, a hinge pin or an eyebolt or something else." She sent a resentful glance Ariel's way. "If little Miss Snoopy-Pants here hadn't been waiting with that camera of hers, I'd have been on my way by now and you wouldn't have missed a thing."

"Why don't you go out at night?" Jill asked her.

Dot huddled down into the chair again. After a moment, when nobody else spoke, she said, "It's—it's not safe. You wouldn't understand."

Ben glanced at Jill. Then, to Dot: "I don't know about that. What would you say if I told you that we've had plates jumping off the table and pictures falling off the walls?"

Dot flinched as though she'd been slapped, but said nothing.

"Mrs. Kellinger," Ariel ventured, "you're talking about witchcraft, aren't you?"

In a sudden hissing whisper: "Don't say that! Don't you know any better? You don't ever talk about that." She turned to Ben, went on in a more normal voice. "If that—that kind of thing's happening, you've got to get out of here right now. Pack your things and leave as soon as you can. Don't wait any longer than you have to. There's been others who stayed and nothing good happened to them."

"Others?" said Ben. "Tell me about them."

Dot gave him a hard look, said nothing.

Jill lifted the gold coin. "You know, it occurs to me that we might be able to make a deal. You need this. We need to know some things. Tell us about the others."

Dot glanced from one of them to the other, her lips pressed taut. Then: "Promise me you won't say a word of this to anyone in this part of the county. Anywhere else, that's your business, but—" Her voice caught. "Not here."

They all promised, and she went on. "Ever since Glen died, every time that widow of his rents this place out, bad things happen to the people who rent it. It's happened something like a dozen times now to different people. Some of them took sick something terrible, and some of them had the worst sort of bad luck, and some of them had things like—like you said— and not one of them did well. Not one. There's been months and months when nobody would take the place at all and she didn't make a cent. Serves her right."

"Why would it serve her right?" Ben asked at once.

Dot was silent for a moment, then went on in a low angry voice. "She should have rented her acreage to Bill and me once Glen died. She should have kept it in the family. Osborne had enough of a farm to keep his family comfortable, but Bill and me only got half of that, and it was the half with the poorer soil. We'd have paid her as much as the Northams do and we'd be doing fine, instead of just barely getting by. But she always hated us. She hated all of Glen's family. She treated poor Josie, that's Glen's daughter by his first wife Cindy, so bad she ran away years ago, and she's always treated Bill and me like dirt."

"Mrs. Kellinger," Ariel asked, "do you know if she treats anyone else that way?"

That got her a sharp look from Dot. "I wouldn't trust her to treat anyone the way she should." Then, her face hardening:

"But I don't know. I've got better things to do with my time than keep track of that nasty creature."

"Somebody's doing the stuff people here don't talk about," Ariel said. "Any idea who?"

Dot looked at the floor, and her shoulders hunched up. "I don't know," she said. "I don't know about things like that."

Ben and Jill looked at each other, said nothing. A moment passed, and then Ben took the gold coin and said, "Mrs. Kellinger, I'm going to give you this, but I'm going to make sure we keep copies of the photos that Ariel took. If it turns out you lied to us, I can think of a couple of people who might get copies of those, starting with your sister-in-law."

Dot's gaze, furious, shot up to his face. "I'm not a goddamned liar," she snapped. "I told you the truth, and if I wasn't a lady I'd tell you what you can do with your goddamned photos."

Ben gave her a long steady look, and then nodded, and handed her the coin. She clutched it in both hands, then muttered "Thank you" and stuffed the coin into her purse. She drew in a breath, then said, "Do you want anything else from me?"

Ben and Jill looked at each other again, and then Jill looked at Ariel, who shook her head slightly. "No," said Jill. "Thank you for the information."

Dot stood up. "You should get out of here before anything else bad happens to you," she said. "There, I've given you good advice. Up to you what you do with it." She turned sharply away and stalked out of the room. Ben got to his feet and followed her. Ariel watched them go, waited for the muffled sounds of the front door opening and closing.

Ben came back into the parlor a few moments later. "Well," he said. "That was—interesting. Thank you, Ariel. That really worked well. I hope you didn't mind too much getting called Little Miss Snoopy-Pants."

"Nope," Ariel said at once, grinning. "I'm going to get a tee shirt that says that." Jill tried to choke back a laugh, with no noticeable success.

"The question," said Ben, ignoring her, "is what we should do now."

"Well," Ariel said, "I think maybe we should check the basement. I want to be sure she didn't move any of the talismans, and we should probably find out if she was telling the truth when she said that was the last of the gold coins. Then I've got a long text to send."

Ben nodded. "That makes sense. You want to go down there now?"

The three of them filed down the stairs into the basement, Jill armed with a big flashlight. Its light glinted gray on all four of Dr. Moravec's talismans, still safely in the corners of the room. When Ariel crouched down, got under the workbench, and shone the light up on the wall where she guessed Dot Kellinger could have reached, she caught sight of a black space between two stones that turned out to be a little recess, large enough to hold a dozen or so coins like the one Dot had dropped. It was empty.

"A 1922 twenty-dollar double eagle," Jill said a few minutes later. They were up in the parlor again. "Of course it's worth a lot more than twenty dollars these days—something like two thousand dollars, I think. But her story checks out. Lots of people kept gold coins stashed away before 1933, when Roosevelt ordered everyone to turn in all their gold to the government, and some people didn't obey the new law once it was passed. I knew an old woman in Monterey who still had half a dozen gold eagles, ten-dollar coins, that her grandmother kept hidden away somewhere in 1933."

Ariel nodded, sipped tea, and said nothing.

"Yeah," said Ben. "The problem is that none of it gets us closer to figuring out what's behind the things that happened to us here. I thought for sure we were going to catch the perp red-handed, and then—" He gestured, palms up. "It turns out she was after a gold coin instead."

"It was interesting," Jill said, "the way she reacted when you mentioned witchcraft, Ariel. She knows a lot more about it than she lets on."

"The question is how much more," said Ben.

That got a moment of perfect silence. Ariel didn't have to guess what they were thinking, for she'd been thinking the same thing herself: Dot Kellinger knew more about witchcraft than she wanted to admit, and she had a serious grudge against her sister-in-law. Something Dr. Moravec had said as they drove up Old Federal Pike on the way to their first visit to the farm whispered itself through Ariel's thoughts: "So there's always the temptation to turn to some secret way of getting back at the people you hate."

She pulled the phone out of her pocket, woke it. "I'm going to go ahead now and text Dr. Moravec," she said. "And after that—"

The next step: that had been on her mind the whole time, once she was sure that Dot Kellinger hadn't come to disrupt the protective spell Dr. Moravec had cast. Waiting around for something else to happen didn't seem like a good use of her time just then, and that left one option she could think of.

"You said it's a pretty easy walk to Criswell, didn't you?" she said to Jill. "I think that's the next place I want to look."

# CHAPTER 10

# THE RIBBON AND THE THORNS

O
utside the day had turned hot and sultry. The driveway of the Kellinger farm hadn't seemed that long when Ariel had driven up and down it in the Buick, but on foot it seemed to stretch on and on. The raven didn't appear, which was some comfort, but the Witch's Wood loomed close to her left, a tangled darkness of twisted pines. Ariel gave it an uneasy glance and kept walking.

Directly ahead was Oscar Bremberg's house, with an antique car she didn't recognize parked in the driveway and the garage door open. As she got closer, she spotted a man in jeans and a stained tee shirt crouching beside the car, doing something to one of the hubcaps. Oscar Bremberg? By the time she'd reached the road he'd gone back into the garage, come out with a toolbox, opened the hood and gotten busy with the engine, confirming it. He glanced up at one point, spotted her, watched her for a few moments, and then turned back to his work.

Ariel considered crossing the street and trying to talk to him. Lord Peter Wimsey would have done it, she told herself, but just then that wasn't as convincing an argument as it should have been. She'd laughed it off, but Dot's snarled comment about Little Miss Snoopy-Pants still stung, and though she meant to keep snooping she couldn't work up the courage just then to do it with a middle-aged man who'd made himself so unpleasant to Jill. Instead, she turned east and started walking along the gravel margin of Lafayette Road, between the pavement and the ditch a yard away from it, toward the dim uncertain shapes of Criswell off in the middle distance.

A few minutes of walking took her past the end of the Witch's Wood and brought Dot and Bill Kellinger's house and barn into sight. Those were just as rundown as she remembered, badly in need of paint and minor repairs. The space between the buildings and the road was in pasture, and six cows loitered not far from the fence, munching grass. They looked reasonably healthy, at least to Ariel's unpracticed eye, and ignored her with a calm placidity that suggested they weren't especially worried or stressed. Did that mean anything? She wasn't sure. Another few minutes and she was past the driveway to the house and barn, and from that point on the fields stretched away unbroken to Criswell.

Some German philosopher or other, one of her high school teachers had claimed, used to insist that the only ideas that matter are the ones that turn up while walking. That seemed like a good theory to put to the test just then, but as far as Ariel could tell, the ideas refused to cooperate. Part of the problem, she realized after a moment, was that her ideas of the kind of person who would use evil magic had too much in common with storybook villains like Lord Roderick Dudgeon in the Bertie Scrubb novels. Those characters were evil because the authors decided they were evil, or because they were the kind of people the authors thought were evil, not because they were driven by the kind of simmering grudges Ariel had glimpsed in Dot Kellinger's eyes. She briefly imagined a Bertie Scrubb story in which it turned out that Mabel Figworthy was an intolerable bully and Bertie himself a priggish little brat, and Lord Dudgeon's wrath, nasty as it might be, was at least partly justified by the circumstances. That made her laugh, but it didn't get her any closer to a solution to the mystery Jill and Ben faced.

She started again, trying to rule out anything that smacked too much of Dudgeon Hall, but that effort didn't work much better. She could line up the little she knew in neat columns—people who had grudges, people who'd acted suspiciously, people who might know about witchcraft—but she didn't have any way to exclude anyone from any of those columns. It occurred to her in a dispiriting moment that she couldn't absolutely rule out Jill and Ben, for that matter. What if one of them didn't really want to be the width of the continent away from their friends and usual haunts in San Francisco, and was faking witchcraft, or actually practicing it, to get the other to agree to break the lease and go back home?

Gravel crunched beneath her shoes. She kept walking, and Criswell came close with glacial slowness.

When she finally got to the little village, it didn't look any more impressive than it had out the window of Dr. Moravec's Buick. The post office and the fire station were bland rectangular brick structures with concrete cornices and arched windows, a little too fussy and a little too aged to pass for products of postwar sprawl. Between them was a pair of nondescript commercial buildings with glass fronts, one housing the Criswell General Store, the other empty and festooned with two SPACE FOR LEASE signs, one in each window. On the far side of the fire station rose the most generic church Ariel thought she'd ever seen, a plain white clapboard structure with a double door facing the street and a squat steeple above it, with a bell for show and loudspeakers to do the actual work. On the far side of the post office were two houses and then fields stretching away into the distance. There was also, unexpectedly, a bus stop with the logo of the Adocentyn bus system on the sign.

The other side of the street featured four houses, a gas station with a mini-mart attached, and a fast-food place that had somehow lingered from the age before franchises. Its faded sign displayed the words EDDIE'S BURGERS and a cartoon bull standing on its hind legs, wearing a tee shirt and a chef's hat as it brandished a plate with a burger on it. Ariel considered the sign, choked back a laugh, and went that direction. The thought of something to drink had a definite appeal just then after a tolerably long and dusty walk. Besides, she told herself, I'm supposed to watch and listen and ask questions. Maybe there'll be someone there to talk to.

She was in luck. The lobby of Eddie's Burgers was empty, but there was a line of stools up against the counter and one bored employee killing time behind it: a boy a few years older than she was, with brown hair, a big Adam's apple, and a plastic name tag pinned to his shirt saying HI, I'M ALEX! Once she perched on one of the stools, he came over with a menu, took her order, got her a soda, and then ventured, "You know, I don't think I've seen you around before."

She aimed a smile at him. "Nope. I'm staying with my cousin and her husband a mile up Lafayette Road, just for a few days. Criswell looks like kind of a nice place."

"Could have fooled me," he said with a wry look.

Ariel stifled a laugh behind one hand. "You're local?"

"No, I catch the bus out here five days a week from my folks' place in Elmhurst." It took her a moment to recognize that as the name of a suburb she'd seen listed on a sign along Old Federal Pike. "It's a job."

"Not too bad a job, I hope."

"Nah, just kind of dull."

It wasn't much of an opening, but she seized it. "I bet. I heard from one of the neighbor ladies that it doesn't stay dull enough where my cousin lives. She's renting the old Kellinger place, 6115 Lafayette Road. You heard anything about that?"

"The Kellinger farm? Oh, yeah. It's got a reputation. I've been working here two and a half years and I've seen, what, three different renters get run out of there."

Ariel didn't have to fake surprise. "Seriously? What happened?"

He shrugged. "I don't know. None of the locals want to talk about it. There was one time, this was last year, the couple who were renting the place then stopped here to get lunch, and they looked really freaked out. Asked me some really weird questions about spooky stuff: witches, curses, that kind of thing. I figured it was bad drugs, or maybe they read too many of those kid's books, I forget the name, the one with the talking wallabies—"

"Bertie Scrubb."

"That's the one." He shrugged. "I don't believe in any of that stuff, you know? But I think a lot of people around here do. Go figure." With a shake of his head: "Maybe it's just because people get sick up that way a lot."

"Sick how?" Ariel asked.

He shrugged again. "Nobody says much about it to a kid from Elmhurst. All I know is what the old folks say to each other when they get coffee here in the morning: 'You hear little Bessie Cray's sick again? Yeah, it's terrible bad.' That kind of stuff."

She made a little more conversation but didn't get anything else useful, and once she finished her drink she got up and headed for the door, promising to stop in again if she had time before she left. Alex said something vaguely hopeful and then settled back into a bored slump by the cash register, waiting for the next customer.

Once she was outside, Ariel found a spot out of sight of the burger place's windows, got out her cell phone, and typed out a fast summary of what Alex had said. That went off to her grandfather, and she stood there for a few minutes, thinking.

So Dot Kellinger hadn't been making up stories when she'd talked about troubles with the Kellinger farm's earlier tenants! That was worth knowing, and if the sickness Alex had mentioned wasn't just a coincidence, there might be something more general at work. If it was someone living, Ariel decided, it certainly looked as though they had it in for Olive Kellinger. But it might not be someone living. And in that case—

In that case, she knew, one thing she needed to do was find someone who might tell her a little more about old Hepzibah Rewell. The post office and the fire station didn't seem promising, and she'd already tried Eddie's Burgers. The General Store looked like the most likely prospect remaining. Ariel put a moment into deciding what to say, crossed the street to the drab little building that housed it, and went to the door.

Inside, though plate glass windows faced the street, the glare of the day seemed far off. Well-used shelves proffered an unlikely mix of snack foods, hardware, and dollar-store bargains. Fluorescent lamps overhead struggled with the dimness and mostly failed, while an elderly air conditioner off where Ariel couldn't see it serenaded her with a chorus of not-quite-rhythmic wheezing noises. The sales counter sprawled up front, close to the door. Sitting behind it, a plump old man with wire-rimmed glasses and a thin scattering of white hair glanced up from a paperback novel, sent a practiced smile her way, and then returned to his book when she didn't approach him at once.

She went deeper into the store, passed a first aid and health care section well stocked with bandages and over-the-counter pills and cheap rubber gloves, and found herself in the stationery department. There the shelves held boxes of envelopes, packages of cheap pens, stacks of little spiral-bound notepads, and plenty more of the same old-fashioned gear. The notepads caught her eye. Newspaper reporters and private eyes in the 1920s fiction she favored, lacking smartphones and text files, were always pulling one of those and a pen out of their pockets to take notes. It occurred to her then that if she ever got rid of her cell phone she could do the same thing. Photos would be harder—did they even make plain cameras any more?

She stopped with a little choked laugh, realizing that she was trying to distract herself from the job she'd come there to do. Gathering her courage, she left the stationery department and went to the front counter.

The old man glanced up at her with the same smile. "Can I help you?" he asked.

"Please," said Ariel. "I wonder if you could tell me where I could find the grave of Hepzibah Rewell."

Pale eyes behind the glasses regarded her. "Blessing, or cursing?"

Nonplussed, Ariel improvised. "Blessing."

"Why, that's very good to hear." The old man reached under the counter and did something there that made a soft tearing noise. His hand returned to the top of the counter a six-inch length of white cloth ribbon. "That'll be twenty-five cents," he said.

She found a quarter in her purse and set it on the counter. He smiled, handed her the ribbon, took the coin, and said, "Go past the fire station and then turn to your right, just this side of the church. Turn left once you get past the church and you'll be on the old road. Another two blocks down that and you'll be at the old cemetery—you can't miss it. Look for the thorn tree with the other ribbons. You can't miss that, either, and her gravestone is right under it."

She thanked him. He smiled, nodded, and went back to his book, as clear a dismissal as though he'd told her to get lost. With an inward shrug, she left the store with the ribbon in her hand. Once outside, she slipped it into her purse and started toward the fire station.

Criswell drowsed in the afternoon heat, and if anybody else was awake in the little town they weren't showing themselves. Ariel went past the fire station and found a narrow track that seemed to head off toward nowhere in particular. She started down it, turned left once she was past the far end of the church, and found herself on a dirt road between two rundown wooden fences. That was promising, and it helped that there was no one in sight and no windows overlooking the dirt road, except for five stained glass windows on the near side of the church.

More promising still was the old cemetery, which came into view almost at once: a fenced-in area with a scattering of old trees and the gray weathered shapes of tombstones from earlier centuries. Around it, vacant lots that might once have held buildings stretched east to the church, west to a fence that marked the beginning of a cornfield, and south to the ditch alongside Lafayette Road.

Sometime in the nineteenth century, she guessed, someone had put in two stone gateposts and a wrought iron gate at the entrance to the cemetery. The posts were still there, thick gray shapes rising up four feet or so to shapeless tops well blotched with lichen, but the gate was reduced to a few scraps of rusted metal that didn't bar anyone's way. Ariel went in, looked around. The cemetery wasn't completely untended—someone had been there with a weed cutter a few weeks back, maybe— but most of the tombstones were broken or fallen over and nearly all of them were illegible.

The clerk at the store was right, though. An old twisted hawthorn tree stood over to one side of the cemetery, berries dangling from its twigs here and there, long thorns guarding them. Ariel spotted the little limp shapes of ribbon hanging here and there from its lower branches as soon as she looked that way.

There was only one tombstone under the tree, and it lay flat on the ground, face up. Ariel walked over to it, examined it. Somebody not too many years back had used paint to trace out the weathered lettering of the name HEPZIBAH REWELL, and below that, barely legible even with the paint, OBIT 1723. Around it, scattered across the grass that covered the grave, were little scraps of once-white cloth and bits of green plastic: artificial flowers, Ariel realized after a moment, left there to the mercies of the weather.

She considered the grave for a long moment, wondering about the flowers, then glanced up as a stray puff of breeze moved past. The ribbons tied to the branches fluttered aimlessly in response. There were maybe thirty of them, and most were bleached and frayed as though they'd been there for years: some were grayish white, some a faint pink that had probably been red once. A few might have been more recent, but only one looked new: a ribbon the vivid red of fresh blood, tied to a low branch exactly above the inscription on the tombstone.

She considered that, too, for another long moment. She hadn't intended to make a wish of her own, she'd taken the ribbon only because the clerk so obviously expected her to, but as she stood there it occurred to her that there might be a point to asking the witch of Criswell Village for help. She looked around, feeling vaguely embarrassed, then reached into her purse and extracted the white ribbon.

At that moment a heavy beating of wings broke the stillness of the afternoon. Ariel looked up reflexively as a black shape came to a halt in the upper branches of the hawthorn. An instant later a big raven perched there. It tilted its head one way and then the other, looking at her with each of its eyes in turn, and waited.

Ariel stared at the bird, swallowed, then said aloud, "Goody Rewell, the people who are renting the farm west of where you used to live are having all kinds of trouble with witchcraft. Somebody I met thinks it's you, but I don't think that's true. If—if it is you, can you let us know what to do so you're satisfied and don't have to keep breaking plates and things? And if it isn't, can you help us find out who's doing it and how to stop it? Thank you."

She had to strain to reach the branches, but managed it, and tied the white ribbon a few inches away from the red one, on the same branch. Once she'd gotten the knot tied, the raven made a croaking sound that reminded her uncomfortably of a laugh, and then spread its wings and flew off with slow heavy wingbeats. She watched it go, then glanced around to see if anyone but the raven had noticed her.

The dirt road and the vacant lots around it were still reassuringly empty. She got out her phone, took pictures of the thorn tree with the ribbons and Goody Rewell's grave, and sent them to her grandfather with a quick note explaining what had happened at the Criswell General Store. Once that was on its way, she tucked the phone back into her purse and turned to go.

Just past the gate, as though materialized out of thin air, someone stood on the old dirt road just outside the cemetery, as if waiting for her.

# CHAPTER 11

# THE SHADOWS OF THE WOOD

Ariel realized at once that there was no point in trying to hide, and there was nothing to hide behind if she'd wanted to make the attempt. She decided to brazen it out. She walked straight out through the gate toward the newcomer, put on a smile as she walked, and said, "Hi."

The person outside the gate was a woman in her thirties in plain farm country clothing, worn jeans and a blue short-sleeved blouse. Lean and rawboned, she had a mop of dull black hair, gray eyes, and an ugly livid scar crossing the left side of her face. She regarded Ariel with what looked uncomfortably like an air of veiled amusement. "Hi," she said. "You're not local, are you? Don't think I've seen you around."

"Nope," said Ariel. "My cousins are renting the Kellinger farm and I'm staying with them for a few days." She put out her hand. "My name's Ariel."

The woman shook the hand. "Suzanne."

"The one who's staying across the road with Mr. Bremberg?"

The look of veiled amusement showed again. "That's farm country for you—everyone knows everyone else's business. Yeah, that's me." Then, considering her: "Not a lot of people outside this area know about Goody Rewell."

"I didn't know that," said Ariel. "Mrs. Kellinger at the farm told me a little about her."

"Did she." The words weren't a question. "That's interesting."

"Not about the ribbons or anything, but I got curious." Ariel put on a smile she didn't feel. "One of the neighbors called me Little Miss Snoopy-Pants, and she's right."

That earned a dry little chuckle. "Someone used to call me that, a long time ago. But you found out enough to go tie a ribbon on the tree above Goody Rewell's grave."

"I read about someone doing that in a book," said Ariel, "and the clerk at the general store knew which kind of ribbon to sell me."

"Chuck Glaser knows more than just about anyone else in town." She tilted her head to one side, considering, and then said: "Any chance you're headed back to the Kellinger farm? This road runs right past it, and I'm going the same way, or mostly."

There might be good reason not to accept the offer, Ariel knew, but she couldn't think of a graceful way to turn it down. "Sure," she said. "I think I came most of the way out this same road this morning on horseback."

Something shifted in the woman's face, back behind the slight smile and the gray impenetrable eyes. "It's the same road." She motioned off to the west, where the hills rose up dim in the afternoon haze, and the two of them started walking.

"You had a favor to ask from Goody Rewell," Suzanne said.

"Yes, I did," said Ariel. Forcing a laugh: "I didn't see you watching, but I guess you saw me, didn't you?"

"I went to the post office to send a package, and when I came out I saw you leave the general store with something that looked like a bit of white ribbon."

"You've got good eyes," said Ariel.

"Runs in the family. But that's what made me curious. Everyone around here knows about Goody Rewell's grave, though you won't find one person in twenty who's gone ahead and tied a ribbon there."

"Are there lots of customs like that around here?"

That got her a cool assessing look. "Not that I ever heard of. I haven't been here that long, though."

Ariel nodded and let the matter drop. They walked on. Ahead, a blur of greenery sorted itself out into the rowan grove by the ruins of the Kellinger mansion.

"I'm guessing that kind of thing interests you," said Suzanne then.

"Well, kind of," Ariel said. "I read the Bertie Scrubb books when I was a kid. I guess everyone does."

"Oh, really," Suzanne said, in a perfect Mabel Figworthy voice. Ariel choked with laughter, and Suzanne chuckled as well. "I was a little old for that kind of thing when the first one came out," she went on, "but I read it, yeah. I just hope you don't think Lord Roderick Dudgeon's evil hedgehogs are spying on us from the hedgerows."

"Nope," said Ariel, with another laugh. "There aren't any hedgerows here."

"True. Or hedgehogs." A few paces further: "And the only thing even a little like Dudgeon Hall burned to the ground a long time ago."

"The old Kellinger mansion? Cousin Jill says that's right up ahead."

"She knows her local history. Yeah, that's what's left of it."

Ariel considered her. "Did any of the Kellingers get into—" She caught herself just in time to avoid mentioning witchcraft. "I don't know, the sort of thing Lord Dudgeon does, but without the hedgehogs?"

That earned her another long assessing look. "Not that I heard," Suzanne said again. "They had some dealings with old Hepzibah Rewell, but that was a long time ago, back in colonial times. No, if you want to know about somebody casting nasty spells, you'll have to look somewhere else."

Ariel considered that as they walked on, and decided to take a risk. "I figured it was worth asking," she said, "because I think someone be doing something like that to my cousins."

"Now why do you think that?" Suzanne asked, after a moment of dead silence.

"Funny stuff happening," said Ariel. "Pictures falling off the walls. Plates falling off the table. Something walking through the halls at night that sounds like this." She scuffed her feet on the dirt road as she walked, glancing Suzanne's way as she did it.

Not a muscle moved in the woman's face. "That's really odd."

"I know. That's why I wondered if something spooky might be going on." Ariel shrugged. "And the local people won't talk about that at all."

Unexpectedly, Suzanne let out a harsh laugh. "No," she said. "No, you can bet on that." She stopped abruptly, turned to face Ariel, and said in a low hard voice: "I'll give you some advice to pass onto your cousins. The best thing for them is to get out, right away. Out of the house, out of the area, out of the state if they can, and take anyone and anything that matters to them. If that kind of thing's happening, every day they stay, they're risking real trouble, the kind that could end up with one or both of them dead. Tell them that. Do you understand?"

"I'll tell them," said Ariel.

Suzanne turned away just as abruptly and started walking again. Ariel caught up with her and walked alongside her.

Moments passed, and then Suzanne said, "You know more than you let on."

"Why do you say that?" Ariel asked.

"You didn't argue. Most people would."

"Maybe I'm just polite."

Suzanne sent a glance her way, followed it with a little derisive chuckle. "No. Are you going to tell me what you know?"

"If you do, will you tell me what you know?" Ariel asked at once.

"No," said Suzanne.

They walked on in silence. The rowan grove and the scattered stones of the burnt mansion went past, and if Suzanne paid the least attention to them Ariel saw no sign of it. A stray breeze set the corn on either side of the road to rustling. Off to the left, the roof of Dot and Bill Kellinger's barn loomed up above the cornstalks, and beyond it the Witch's Wood rose up dark and uncommunicative.

"I get the sense," Ariel said then, "that there's a lot going on here that I'll never know anything about."

"Yeah. That's farm country for you."

"That doesn't help my cousins any," Ariel pointed out.

"I've already told you what they've got to do," said Suzanne. "And here's some advice for you, too. You know something about this business, but not enough to stay out of trouble, not by half. If you're smart, Little Miss Snoopy-Pants, you'll stay out of all this and go back home as soon as you can. Otherwise you may just get hurt."

Ariel gave her a wary look. "Is that a warning or a threat?"

Amusement showed again in the other woman's eyes. "You decide."

The Witch's Wood was close by then, and the fence on that side of the road sagged where the cornfield ended and the first straggling pines began. Suzanne veered over to the place where the boards dipped lowest, and turned to face Ariel. "Here's where you go your way and I go mine. Tell your cousins what I said, and think about it yourself, too."

She climbed easily over the sagging boards and headed off along the narrow gap between the corn and the trees. Ariel watched her go. A sudden flapping of wings caught her attention and she turned, looking up into the pines. Something had flown from tree to tree. The raven? She couldn't tell.

When she glanced back the way Suzanne had gone, there was no trace of anyone.

Ariel stood there for a moment, startled, then shook her head. Memory stirred: she'd looked around when she'd left the general store, and seen no one, nor anyone approaching the cemetery. Magic, she thought. Maybe. The afternoon brought her no answers, and she started down the last stretch of road alone.

The Witch's Wood ran alongside the road most of that distance. Ariel considered it as she walked. Somewhere past those dark trees and dense shadows, she thought, was a little pond, and near it was the place where Hepzibah Rewell lived and worked her witchcraft, and people came to ask for her help. She tried to imagine the fields around her as they were back in Goody Rewell's day, when the forest still stretched all but unbroken in every direction, when Criswell was a little cluster of new houses huddled together on the edge of the unknown and the west wind that blew over Norton Hill came sweeping across country no white people had ever seen. The twisted pines to her left seemed to cling to some memory of those days. Was that why the witch of Criswell Village had charged Josiah and Priscilla Tibbetts to keep the wood inviolate? The trees offered no answers either.

A few more minutes brought Ariel to the pasture gate, and from there it was an easy walk to the farmyard and the barn. The porch of the Northams' house was empty when she started that walk, but she was only a few yards across it when a woman in a light green sun dress came out and stood there facing the Kellinger farm. Ariel kept a sidelong watch on her as she crossed the pasture and went into the barnyard on the other end.

The barn door was half open, but when she got close enough to see through it she spotted Ricky inside, busy doing something with the horses: good reason not to go through. Instead, Ariel veered around the east side of the barn, close to Olive Kellinger's cottage. Olive herself was sitting on her porch, writing something. She glanced up as Ariel passed by and said, "Oh, Ariel? Might I ask you for a favor?"

Ariel turned and crossed to the porch. "Hi, Mrs. Kellinger. What is it?"

The old woman beamed up at her and finished writing. "If you could take this to Ben," she said, holding out a square of paper, "that would spare me a walk. He picks up my groceries for me when he goes into town. Such a pleasant young man."

"Sure," Ariel told her, and took it.

"Oh, thank you. Did you have a good time riding Corazon this morning? I was glad to see her getting a little more exercise—her owner can only get out here on weekends, you know."

"I had a great time. It's been a couple of years since I had the chance to go riding."

"Well, I'm glad. I hope you'll have another chance while you're here."

Ariel said something suitable in response and headed for the kitchen door. A glance at the square of paper showed an ordinary grocery list. The notepaper was decorated across the top with a line of the same white geese wearing blue gingham bonnets the old woman had on her porch furniture and her curtains.

Inside the house, Ben took the list and thanked her. "What is it with the geese?" she asked him, indicating the note.

He laughed and shrugged. "Those used to be fashionable, like those black and white cows you used to see everywhere. Olive likes them. If you ever get a look inside her cottage, they're everywhere—curtains, wall art, the towels in the kitchen, you name it."

He went back to work on dinner, and Jill was busy in her studio with a painting, so Ariel had the parlor to herself. She settled down on the sofa, got out her phone, and checked for messages. All she'd gotten was a brief text from her grandfather thanking her for the information she'd sent, and nothing else.

She frowned at that, hoping that he wasn't angry at her for some reason, and set to work writing up a detailed report on what she'd learned in Criswell, her conversation with Suzanne, and the odd way Suzanne had appeared and disappeared.

Once that was on its way, she tried to lose herself in a story, but her mood turned restless. After a while she put the e-reader away, pocketed her phone and went back outside. The heat of the day was fading out as the sun headed west. The barn was closed up again but the sound of hoofbeats and a voice came from the pasture, and when Ariel went that way she found Ricky working with Stormalong. She had him on a twenty-foot rope—a few minutes passed before she remembered the right word, "longe"—and was working on his gaits, calling out "walk," "trot," "canter," and "gallop" by turns, pivoting as he moved in a circle around her. Ariel went over to the edge of the pasture, climbed up on the fence next to the gate and sat there watching.

After five minutes or so Stormalong looked winded. Ricky walked him slowly around the pasture for a while to let him catch his breath, praising him, and then walked him back toward the barn. She gave Ariel a startled look as she came close; Ariel guessed that she hadn't noticed her there at all.

"Hi," said Ariel. "You're good at that."

Ricky mumbled something that was probably "Thank you." In a clearer voice: "Corazon likes you."

"Well, I like her," said Ariel. "So it's mutual."

That got her a little lopsided smile. "You can help out if you want."

"Sure," said Ariel. "Just tell me what you want me to do." She slid down from the fence and followed Ricky and Stormalong to the barn.

Corazon certainly looked happy to see Ariel, though another carrot from the bin didn't exactly hurt their relationship. The mare had already gotten her exercise and been curried and brushed down; Ariel could tell that at a glance, so she got a bucket of water for Stormalong and then started cleaning his saddle and tack while Ricky took care of the gelding.

"You've been doing this for a long time," Ariel said, after she hefted the saddle up onto the beam where it was stored.

To her surprise, Ricky gave her a broad grin. "Yeah. Since I was little." The grin faltered. "I want a place of my own and a whole bunch of horses to take care of. Someday." She put the curry comb away and got out a stiff-bristled brush.

The whole time while they worked, Ariel wondered what Ricky knew about witchcraft and the strange events at the farm, but she knew better than to think she could bring the subject up just then. Later, she told herself. Maybe.

To her surprise, Ricky forestalled her. Once they'd finished getting Stormalong and his saddle and tack dealt with, wished the horses a good night, and walked to the back door of the barn, Ricky turned to her and said, "You staying here tonight?" When Ariel nodded, she hunched her shoulders and said, "Just be careful, okay?"

They went into the farmyard. Ariel asked, "Careful of what?"

Ricky looked away, and her shoulders hunched up further. "Just be careful. I wouldn't spend the night here for anything."

Ariel turned toward her, trying to think of the right question to ask. Before she could find the words, another voice sounded over toward the woodlot: Olive Kellinger's, saying "Oh, another one, that's bad," in a distressed tone. Ariel turned to look and saw the old woman coming out of her cottage, shaking her head. She turned back to ask Ricky to wait a moment, but the other girl had ducked back into the barn. A moment later the barn door shut with a bang.

Stifling her irritation—she was certain that she could have learned something from Ricky given a few more minutes of talk—Ariel crossed the farmyard to Olive's cottage. "What is it?"

The old woman looked up in surprise. "Oh, Ariel! I didn't know you were still out here. It's just—" Her hands gestured helplessness. "A lovely old plate I've had for years jumped right off the table and broke in pieces. It's been weeks since I've had anything like that happen, and I'd hoped that Goody Rewell's ghost had settled down." Then, obviously worried: "I hope you didn't go into the woodlot or anything."

"No, I didn't," Ariel said, with perfect honesty.

"Well, that's something. I wanted to tell—"

Just then an engine started up on the other side of the farmhouse. Ariel glanced that way. A compact pickup lurched into motion and headed down the driveway with Ricky behind the wheel, driving fast.

"Poor thing," said Mrs. Kellinger then. "She does such a wonderful job with the horses, but she's afraid of the oddest things and she believes all kinds of superstitions. Well." She shook her head. "I wanted to tell Jill and Ben to be careful. When this kind of thing happens to me, sometimes it happens to other people too."

"Mrs. Kellinger," Ariel said then, "do you know if there's anybody alive around here who does things like that? Somebody who might have a grudge or something?"

Mrs. Kellinger glanced up. "Now where did you get that notion?"

"I read about that kind of thing in a book," said Ariel.

"Oh, I hope not. I really do. I've had disagreements with a few people down through the years, but I don't think any of them would lead to that." She shuddered. "I grew up just ten miles from here, you know, and the people in this county are practically family. I can't believe that any of them would do something like that, even if anybody still remembered how."

"It was just a thought," said Ariel, with a shrug. "I can tell Jill and Ben if you like."

"Would you? That would be very kind of you."

"Sure. Do you need any help cleaning up the mess?"

"Thank you, but no," said Mrs. Kellinger. "I've already put the pieces in the garbage. It's sad—that plate was in the family for such a long time." She shook her head again. "Well, Ariel, good night, and don't forget to tell Jill and Ben."

Ariel promised she wouldn't, wished her a good night, and started for the kitchen door.

## CHAPTER 12

# THE WHISPERING FOOTSTEPS

Dinner that night was what people in Summerfield liked to call "fusion cuisine," meaning in this case a free mix of Californian and Vietnamese cooking. Odd though it looked to see enchiladas with fried noodles on the side, Ariel found she liked the result. Once dinner was over, Ben got to work on the dishes and Jill hauled herself to her feet, saying, "You'll have to excuse me. Trash pickup's first thing tomorrow."

"Can I help?" Ariel asked, and got a startled look and then a smile.

That errand took them out the kitchen door into the evening. The sun was down behind Norton Hill but the sky was still light; swallows darted and swooped over the barn, and the sound of a car heading east on Lafayette Road seemed startling against the background quiet. This far out from the city, Ariel didn't expect ordinary garbage and recycle bins, but there they were, parked in a corner behind the house. Ariel took the garbage bin and started rolling it toward the driveway, but stopped when Mrs. Kellinger came out of her cottage with a full trash bag in hand. A glance at Jill told her what she needed to know, and she left the bin, crossed to the cottage, took the flimsy white plastic bag, and got a bright smile and a few words of thanks in trade. The bag went into the bin, where it landed with a squelch, and Ariel got the bin rolling again down toward the driveway.

Once the bins were on the roadside waiting for the pickup, she and Jill headed back up toward the house. The first pale stars were coming out overhead by then, and an owl hooted from somewhere in the Witch's Wood. "I can see why you want to stay here," said Ariel.

"I hope we can," Jill said in a worried tone.

Once that was done with, the three of them settled in the parlor, where Ben put on headphones and watched online news programs on a tablet, Jill buried herself in a fat paperback novel, and Ariel curled up in one corner of the sofa and took a break from detecting with an F. Scott Fitzgerald short story. After an hour or so, when night had settled in to stay outside the windows, Ben took off the headphones and said, "This is when we usually do the evening prayers. If you're not comfortable being part of that, Ariel, don't worry about it."

"I'm fine with it," Ariel told him. "And kind of curious. You'll have to tell me what to do, though."

"It's pretty simple. The altar's in Jill's studio." He got up, Jill put her book aside and stood, and Ariel blanked the screen on her e-reader and followed them into the entry and through it, to the room on the other side. That turned out to be the mirror image of the parlor, with a matching fireplace, and two large easels with half-finished paintings on them over to one side. The room also had a chest-high wooden cabinet up against the wall a few feet from the fireplace, with a yellow curtain hanging from a makeshift curtain rod hiding whatever was on top of it. Ben went to the cabinet and opened the curtain, while Jill stayed back and Ariel copied her.

The top of the cabinet turned out to hold two candlesticks, a bowl full of sand for incense sticks, cups and glasses, flowers and fruit, and a glass-screened oil lamp burning with a steady bright flame. Behind and above the lamp was a small hanging scroll fastened to the wall, and on the scroll was a single eye surrounded by rays of light. Ben got five sticks of incense out from inside the cabinet, stuck their wooden ends into the sand in the bowl, and lit them, while Jill showed Ariel how to fold her hands—the Cao Dai religion did that, but not the way Ariel had learned in her occasional visits to churches back in Summerfield. Then they all bowed three times, knelt on the floor, and bowed many more times as Ben recited prayers in Vietnamese. Jill joined in the prayers a little awkwardly, and Ariel tried to copy their movements and hoped she wasn't doing anything wrong.

Sometimes, on those Sundays when she'd gone with friends to churches in Summerfield, Ariel had sensed someone or something listening to the prayers. It never felt much like the God the preachers talked about, the angry old man in the clouds perpetually shaking a finger at her because she'd done something or other that He didn't like. It felt closer than that, and stranger: wholly other, and yet familiar in a way she could never quite name. She sensed the same presence just then, hovering somewhere nearby in a space she couldn't measure, as Ben's voice moved through many-toned sentences, and she tried more or less successfully to bow her head when he bowed his.

The eye on the hanging scroll looked on with a tremendous calm, as though none of the fears and follies of human beings troubled it in the least. Glimpsing it as she rose from another kneeling bow, Ariel thought of the book she'd glanced through in her grandfather's house just before Jill and Ben had arrived, the engraving of the odd one-stringed instrument fretted with stars and worlds, the hand reaching out from billowing clouds to turn the peg and put the string into tune. The eye and the hand reminded her of each other, and made her think again about the preachers and their God. She'd had the sense for years that they didn't know any more about the presence she'd felt than she did, and might know less. It occurred to her then that someone else, somewhere else, might know more.

Ben finished praying, knelt in silence for a while, and then got to his feet. Jill stood a moment later. It wasn't until Ariel tried to do the same thing that she discovered that her lower legs had fallen asleep. Jill, trying to stifle a smile, caught her arm as she staggered and helped her up. Meanwhile Ben closed the yellow curtain around the altar and turned to them. "Sorry," he said. "If you're not used to kneeling it helps to put a pillow under you."

"I'm okay," Ariel said sheepishly. The feeling of pins and needles in her lower legs argued with her about that, but she was able to walk back to the parlor without too much clumsiness and settled into the corner of the sofa.

"So what did you think of it?" Jill asked then.

"It's interesting," said Ariel. "Can you tell me about the prayers?"

"Sure," said Ben, and launched into a complicated explanation that left Ariel thoroughly confused. She gathered that the first prayer went to the Supreme Being and the others to Buddhas, immortals, and other holy beings, who seemed to be something like the saints her Catholic friends in Summerfield prayed to, but beyond that she quickly lost her way in the intricacies of the Cao Dai teachings. That apparently showed in her face, because Ben stopped, laughed, and said, "I know, there's a lot of it. It seems really simple if you grow up with it."

"For what it's worth," said Jill, "I'm still sorting it all out. Until this whole thing started I didn't give a lot of thought to religion or anything like that, but—" Her shrug finished the sentence: what else can you do?

The rest of the evening was quiet enough. After a little while Ben stood up and said, "Well, that's enough for me. Let me get some tape on a couple of doors and then it's good night, fair ladies." Ariel choked back a laugh, watched him pull a tape dispenser from the little drawer in one of the end tables and head for the kitchen. He was back a few moments later, put the tape away, wished them both a good night, and headed upstairs. Running water gurgled in the pipes for a while. Jill got up next and said, "See you in the morning. I hope everything stays fine." She turned off most of the lights, left one on for Ariel.

"So do I," said Ariel, and listened to her footfalls going up the stairs.

She turned back to F. Scott Fitzgerald then, but for some reason the story couldn't hold her attention. The eye surrounded by light, the hand emerging from clouds: those kept circling back into her thoughts, and after a while she got out her phone and did an internet search for the image of the hand tuning the one-stringed instrument. It took her half a dozen search strings to find it, and several more tries to find out anything about it. When she did, her mouth fell open, because the picture— a monochord, the article called the instrument, tuned by the hand of God—was in a book published in 1617 called *Utriusque Cosmi Historia*, which meant *History of the Two Universes*. It was written by somebody named Robert Fludd, and it was the same book whose pages she'd turned in her grandfather's house.

A moment later, the surprise gave way to something more complex. It shouldn't have startled her, she told herself, that Dr. Moravec had books four hundred years old in his parlor: he was the kind of person who would do that. No, the thing that left her feeling uncomfortable was that she had so little time to turn the pages of those books before her summer vacation was over. Then it would be time to board the train back to Summerfield and two years of community college, trying to prepare for a career or at least a job when she still had no idea what she wanted to do with the rest of her life.

That thought led off in too many directions she didn't want to go. An irritable tap on the phone screen chased off the image from *Utriusque Cosmi Historia*, and another opened a text file. She had plenty of things to pass on to her grandfather, after all.

Half an hour of typing got the details copied down, and another few strokes sent the file to Dr. Moravec. By then she was beginning to feel sleepy. She got up and had just turned toward the entry when an uneasy suspicion surfaced in her mind: if she couldn't trust anyone, could she trust that Ben had really put tape where he'd said he would?

That sent her into the kitchen, phone in hand. The phone's flashlight gave her ample light to glance at the closet and the stair to the basement: yes, both had little pieces of tape between the door and the frame low down, where they wouldn't be spotted at a casual glance. She was about to turn back to the parlor and head for bed when it occurred to her that he could replace the tape just as easily as he'd put it there, if he'd meant to pretend that something disembodied had gotten down into the cellar. Fortunately she remembered a trick from the book on private investigation she'd read. She went back into the parlor, tried the drawer where Ben had gotten the tape, and found a pencil there. That was all she needed, and a moment later she'd written her signature on the tape on the cellar door, lightly, so it couldn't be seen at a glance.

The pencil went back into the drawer. She turned off the light in the parlor, picked her way into the entry and up the stairs mostly by feel, and found her way to the bedroom she'd been given. Fifteen minutes later she'd locked her bedroom door and nestled down under unfamiliar covers, with the lights off and sleep creeping quietly over her.

She slept hard for a while—how long, she could never be sure afterwards. Nor could she tell for certain what waked her. All she knew was that she blinked away suddenly in the darkness, feeling uneasy for no reason she could name.

She lay in the bed for a while without moving. Darkness pressed close about her, fading on one side into a faint pallid presence she couldn't identify at first. Her room in her grandfather's house had a dim yellow glow trickling in from the city lights outside even in the blackest hours before dawn, her room back in Summerfield had orange sodium glare from the streetlamp right outside on Cedar Street splashed in through every little gap in the curtains, but what filtered into her borrowed room that night was scarcely light at all. It was moonlight, she realized finally, from a thin moon not yet far enough around to shine on the window. She guessed that even if she got up and opened the curtains, that wouldn't let in enough light to notice. After a few more minutes, the darkness and the feeling of uneasiness became oppressive enough that she decided to go pull the curtains open anyway.

That was when she realized that she couldn't move.

Panic jabbed at her then. She was lying on her back, the covers half thrown off, and a sense of dreadful vulnerability seized her. She threw all her strength into trying to make any part of her move—a finger, an eyelid—and failed.

Her mind was clear. So were her memories. She knew with cold certainty exactly what would happen next, and it did. A faint sound like shuffling footsteps whispered somewhere in the hallway outside her door. She made another frantic effort to move, with no more result than the first. The footfalls came closer, approaching the door. With them came something else: a sudden unreasoning certainty that she was about to die. Stark terror seized her. She would have screamed and flung herself from the bed if she could have done anything at all.

The toby was still around her neck. She could feel it there, resting over to one side in the hollow in front of her left shoulder, under the tee shirt. She clung to that knowledge, called to mind Aunt Clarice assembling the toby and weaving the spell that had left Ariel's mind baffled for a time. The silver coin was in her purse, on the other side of the room; the pepper was still in her shoes by the foot of the bed; but she had the toby. She hoped it would be enough. Memory brought up the Cao Dai prayers Ben had recited, and she tried in vain to recall even a few of the Vietnamese words. Frantic thoughts tumbled through her mind. Was there anyone she could pray to? Was there anyone who would listen?

Then she felt the thing come into the room.

She couldn't see it in the darkness, and the door hinges made no sound, but she could hear its sliding footsteps as it came toward the bed, and she could feel it: more absence than presence, a gap in existence, opening to swallow her. The dim uncertain moonlight from the window brightened slowly. All at once Ariel could see something dark looming up between her and the window, blotting out the moonlight, bending toward her.

It stopped.

Ariel tried again to move, with no more result than before. She could feel her heart pounding and cold sweat breaking out all over her, but her muscles stayed limp. The thing bent over her, as though straining toward her, but it came no closer.

Moments passed. Then the thing went around to the other side of the bed, making the same whispering footsteps as before, and strained toward her from that direction. Ariel was further from that side, and for a moment she thought the thing would climb onto the bed, but it stopped there, too. After a little while it moved to the foot of the bed, and seemed to recoil from the shoes, as though the pepper Ariel had put in them dismayed it. There it stayed for a time that seemed to stretch on forever, a silent shapeless darkness in the dim moonlight.

Then, as though a switch had been flipped, it disappeared, and Ariel could move again.

She sat up reflexively, gasping and shuddering. Once she had enough presence of mind she reached for her cell phone, fumbled with it, and got the flashlight app to turn on. The light revealed an empty room. After a moment, with an effort, she turned the flashlight off, and listened for the footsteps. Nothing disturbed the hush of the night. Time passed and her heartbeat finished settling back to a normal pace. Finally she lay back down and pulled up the covers.

She didn't expect to get back to sleep at all, not after those minutes of terror, but she could feel tiredness weighing down her body: not the unnatural exhaustion Jill had described on that first morning at Dr. Moravec's house, but the ordinary weight of a busy and strenuous day. Besides, she told herself, whatever the thing was, it couldn't get me. Maybe it was Aunt Clarice's toby that kept it away and maybe it was the Cao Dai prayers, but it couldn't get me.

The words stretched and blurred as sleep took her.

## CHAPTER 13

# *THE COLD BRIGHT STARS*

The cell phone woke Ariel with a few bars of discordant music. She was groggy enough at first that she wondered if she'd set the alarm, then guessed that her grandfather was calling and threw off the covers in a hurry. It wasn't until she sat up that memory stirred, reminded her whose texts that scrap of music heralded. She glared at the phone, took her time rubbing her eyes and stretching, then got up and went to her suitcase to sort out the clothes she meant to wear that day: anything to put off the inevitable for a few more minutes.

That was when memory stirred again, and reminded her what had happened in the middle of the night. She blanched, and went to the door. It was still locked. That set her heart pounding, and she went and sat on the bed for a few moments, staring at nothing she could have named.

Stop it, she told herself. Stop it. It didn't get you. You're not tired the way Jill said she was, and you knew already that this stuff is real. You've seen a ghost, and you've seen Aunt Clarice. Now you've seen a—

Was there a name for the thing that had come walking through a locked door and loomed over her, blotting out the moonlight? She reminded herself to ask her grandfather about that as soon as she could. That made her reach for the phone, because the first thing she needed to do was to let Dr. Moravec know what had happened. She could feel that in her bones. A tap on the screen woke the phone, and she got to work on a text to him.

She was still working on that when the phone in her hands chimed again, a bland inoffensive sound this time. That startled her, and she finished the text to her grandfather, sent it, and checked the inbox. There were two texts waiting for her, the earlier one marked CARMEN MORAVEC-JONES and the later one THEODORE MORAVEC—everybody called her father "Ted," but he clung to the formality of his full name like a drowning sailor to a broken spar. She could guess easily enough what that meant, let out a ragged sigh, and opened her father's text first.

That said exactly what she expected it to say: ARIEL, PLEASE DON'T UPSET YOUR MOTHER. I KNOW SHE'S NOT BEING FAIR BUT YOU HAVE TO REMEMBER HOW MUCH STRESS SHE'S UNDER. BRITNEY SENDS HER BEST. LOVE, DAD. She gave it a long bleak look, then closed it and braced herself. That always meant a tirade from her mother, not just an ordinary lecture but something right off the charts. She paused, opened the other text.

It was as bad as she'd expected. She scrolled down through the whole thing in a spirit of abstract curiosity—six screens without a break—and then went back to the beginning and started reading it. None of it was new, she could have taken the first few words of most of the lines and filled in the rest from memory, from dozens of other texts and from all the fights that they'd had. She knew her mother's facial expressions and the tones of her voice well enough that she could imagine how the words would have come spilling out in person, as her mother whipped herself up into a rage that would give her an excuse to say something unforgivable.

Nor was there any doubt in Ariel's mind what the unforgivable thing would be. After a screen or so she skimmed forward past the overfamiliar words, looking for a name she knew she'd find. It was in the middle of the third screen, then again toward the bottom of that screen, and then over and over again through the next two screens: an ordinary name: DANIEL. The first time it showed up after I KEEP THINKING ABOUT, and after that it came before WOULD HAVE and WOULDNT HAVE and more of the same kind, flinging the name at Ariel over and over again.

A word she didn't normally let herself use forced its way out. The temptation to snap the phone in half surfaced again, but she pushed it aside: not now, she told herself, not when I need it to text and take photos. Instead, she dropped the phone on the bed, flung herself toward the door and got it open. The bathroom door across the hall was open, a small mercy but a welcome one. Ariel ducked across, locked the bathroom door behind her, and shed the tee shirt and panties. A quick twist of the shower tap put it all the way to the cold side, and she stepped in.

Water cold enough to sting struck her like a slap across the face. She stood there gasping for a minute or so while it streamed over her, then turned the shower off and got out. Her skin was a mass of goosebumps—ducklumps, a memory whispered to her, ducklumps, and she didn't wince, even though it was Daniel who'd always called them that. The shock of the cold shower worked its usual magic, handing her back enough self-control that she could let herself remember the phrase without starting to cry.

She toweled herself off hard, leaving her skin red and her hair as jumbled as a fright wig, then skinned back into the panties and tee shirt and recrossed the hall. The cell phone still sat there on the bed where she'd dropped it. She picked it up and jabbed at the screen, shutting it off for the time being. The cell phone went back on the bedside table, and she sat on the bed again and buried her face in her hands, trying not to notice the beautiful summer morning taking shape outside the window.

Of course it was a beautiful summer morning, she thought. It had to be. Like that other morning seven years back. The One Perfect Day, she'd called it afterwards, though a few years further on she'd admitted to herself that there had been other summer days just as perfect, scattered like stray beads across the landscape of her childhood. It was the contrast that made that one day gleam so much more brightly than the others, a crystal shape set close against coal-black midnight.

For it had been a perfect day, right up until the end: a day full of blue skies reaching up to forever, flat-bottomed clouds in great luminous heaps drifting past on winds she couldn't feel, green lawns and green trees and the water-and-chlorine smell of suburban sprinklers, all the familiar sights and sounds of a Summerfield childhood. After a breakfast of cold cereal and banana slices she'd ridden her bike down to Julie and Sophie's house eight blocks away, no particular purpose in mind, just hanging out with her best friends. Later on they'd biked over to a place on Fillmore Avenue called Rudy's where you could get soft-serve ice cream cones in flavors that changed from week to week.

She'd taken her time getting home from there, basking in the golden light of the afternoon, and came up the driveway just in time to say hi to Daniel as he tucked his karate gear into the passenger seat of the old red Nissan he drove. He'd teased her and ruffled her hair, she'd teased him back, and he headed off to the dojo and three hours of hard training, chasing his dream. Going into the house, she'd thought about how much it would hurt when he graduated from high school a year later and went to Japan to get the advanced training he'd need to open a dojo of his own. It never occurred to her that he'd be leaving sooner, or more permanently.

Afternoon turned to evening, family friends came over for a barbecue, and her father got busy at the grill, one of the few places where he shed his usual meekness and took charge of anything. A familiar chorus of scents and tastes brought burgers to the table. Potato chips and cold pop joined them, while the grown-ups chatted aimlessly and she and Britney made faces at each other and laughed. Daniel got back in time to take a folding lawn chair and wolf down three burgers, then went inside. Evening drew on, turning the heat of the charcoal into a dull red glow as it sank toward ash; the first few fireflies danced around the edges of the yard, the stars came out and the guests trickled away. Inside, she'd curled up in a corner of the sofa and read the last four chapters of *The Hound of the Baskervilles* while the television droned on unnoticed, and her mother, equally unnoticed, went over to Daniel, said something about needing to talk, led him into the family room and closed the door.

Ariel hadn't heard the fight. It wasn't Daniel's way to raise his voice. When he left the family room and left the house and climbed into his car, he did it precisely, without unnecessary noise: his anger always showed itself in silence and icy self-control. Her mother had raised her voice toward the end, but by then Ariel was curled up in her bed, dozing off with Nicodemus the wolf guarding her feet, and her mother's voice got loud and shrill often enough, nothing to worry about so long as it wasn't aimed at her.

Then, hours later, her father shook her awake out of dim perplexing dreams, saying something about bad news: a call from the police, she gathered after a moment, a car accident. She was disoriented enough that it took a while for her to fit the pieces together: a cliffside curve on Hilltop Road on the old state highway west of Summerfield, two cars slamming into each other and plunging through the guardrail, the waiting depths of the old Gadsden quarry a hundred feet down, a fireball roiling up toward the cold bright silence of the stars.

One of the cars was Daniel's.

She pieced together the rest of the story over the week or so that followed, as she and the rest of the family stumbled through the unfamiliar routines of dealing with death and the first wrenching grief gave way to a deeper and more paralyzing numbness. She'd listened to her mother complain for most of two years before then that Daniel needed to get serious about life and stop wasting his time with martial arts. She'd heard her mother insist over and over again that it was just a phase, but it must have finally become clear even to her what Ariel had known already for months: that Daniel meant what he'd been saying, that he wasn't interested in college and a respectable business career, that he wanted to go to Japan once he graduated from high school, and teach karate for a living once he came back home.

Something had happened the night before the barbecue, Ariel figured that out within a week or so. It wasn't until most of two months after the crash, when her mother was gone on a business trip and her father drank too much and sat up late at the kitchen table with his face in his hands, crying and mumbling to himself, that she found out what it was. Daniel couldn't pay his dojo fees himself and he couldn't cover the costs of the trip to Japan, not with the job market in the tank the way it was. So their mother had bullied their father into agreeing that there would be no more money for Daniel's martial arts training and no trip to Japan: Daniel was going to act like an adult, be reasonable, and spend his evenings and weekends studying so he could get into a good school and land a corporate job like theirs. That was what she had told Daniel, the night of the barbecue, and that was what had sent him out the door in an icy rage to his car and a one-way drive up Hilltop Road.

That knowledge was the thing that brought Ariel out of overwhelming grief into a bleak but bearable equilibrium. Being able to destroy something is a source of power: she understood that for the first time. She knew with perfect clarity that she could wreck her relationship with her mother irrevocably and tear her entire family apart. All it would take was three simple words said aloud, and repeated whenever she chose. She could sense the power those words gave her in the sudden brittleness that filled the room whenever anyone mentioned Daniel in her mother's presence, in the way the last trace of spirit seemed to trickle out of her father once the funeral was over and the ugly little box of ashes went into the ugly little niche in the

Summerfield cemetery, in the pointless quarrels that drove one wedge after another between her and Britney, and above all in the way that she could face down her mother when it mattered, meeting anything she said with cold silence and an unwavering stare.

Three simple words:

You killed him.

Ariel raised her face from her hands. After a moment she got up, went to the dresser and picked up her cell phone. A tap woke it, showed her mother's text.

It would be the easiest thing in the world. That was the thought that circled through her mind then, as it had so many times before: every time her mother had brought up Daniel in one of their fights, in fact, once his death was far enough in the past that she could pretend that the hard fact of that final quarrel didn't exist, and start transforming him in her imagination into the golden child, the one who would have done everything right that Ariel did wrong. Ariel let herself savor, for just a little while, the thought of saying those words. A few sentences: she knew all the words already, knew exactly where "Daniel" and "you killed him" should go, knew in her bones just what it would feel like to type the words and send them on their way and wait for the response. It would be so very easy.

Instead, she deleted the text from her mother and left it unanswered. She considered doing the same thing to the one from her father, then thought for a little while about sending him a text that read WHY DON'T YOU GIVE HER THAT ADVICE SOMETIME, but that would be pointless, and cruel into the bargain. Even before Daniel's death, he wasn't the kind of man who could stand up to his wife, or for that matter to anyone else. She thought of his plump puzzled face, winced, and pushed that thought aside.

Instead, she typed: DAD—IM STAYING WITH FRIENDS OF GRANDPAS IN THE COUNTRY. IM GOING HORSEBACK RIDING IN

HALF AN HOUR. TELL MOM I KNOW I HAVE TO FIGURE OUT WHAT IM GOING TO DO, OKAY? JUST NOT THIS MINUTE. A

It wasn't what she wanted to say, and she knew as she hit the SEND button that it would probably field her another tirade from her mother. It was still the best she could do. She put the phone down again and started getting ready for the day.

The first clear morning light had begun to sink into summer haziness before Ariel finally went downstairs. Even through the tangle of her own feelings, she could tell at once that something had changed, and not for the better. Jill, sitting on the couch with a book in her lap, looked up as Ariel came into the parlor and confirmed it. "We've got trouble."

"Okay," said Ariel. "What is it?"

"Someone or something must have gotten into the cellar last night. I don't know how. The tape was still there when I got up this morning, but the pressure's back. And—" She swallowed visibly. "I heard the thing in the hallway. The footsteps."

"I know. It tried to get to me." Seeing Jill's face blanch: "I'm okay. It couldn't do anything but scare me."

A frozen moment passed, and then Jill nodded. "Well, that's something. Ben left a message for Dr. Moravec. I don't know if there's anything you want to do."

"Well, let's take a look," said Ariel.

They went into the kitchen, where Ben was working on the dishes and greeted Ariel with a distracted good morning. Ariel said something friendly in response and headed straight for the cellar door. There was still a little piece of tape bridging the gap between door and frame, low down, but something about it didn't look right. Ariel crouched down. The tape didn't have her signature on it, and it looked shinier than the tape she remembered.

She looked up. "Ben, can you get the tape you used last night?"

He gave her a baffled look, but dried his hands, left the sink, came back a moment later with the tape dispenser. Side by side, the difference was obvious. "This isn't the same tape," Ariel said. "Somebody spotted it and replaced it after they went down into the cellar. I can tell you that for sure because I signed my name on the original tape, after you went to bed."

That got her startled looks from both of them. Ben squatted down next to her, looked at the tape on the door and the roll in the dispenser, and said, "Damn. You're right."

"We should probably check the basement," Ariel said. "Let me get my phone first and get some pictures."

She went up the stairs to get the phone, just ahead of Ben. As she left her bedroom again he came through one of the other doors, held up the key, and said, "It was still in the folder and the drawer was locked. I don't know what to make of that." Ariel shrugged and led the way back down the stairs.

Once they went down in the basement, it was clear what had happened. Somebody had gotten in there during the night, that was obvious, and whoever it was had gone digging through the clutter in all four corners to reveal the places where Dr. Moravec had placed the talismans. There were finger marks here and there in the dust, but the flash from her phone camera showed the same featureless prints as before: rubber gloves again, Ariel was sure of it.

"So it's not a ghost," Ben said.

Ariel had been thinking the same thing, word for word. "Nope." She got to her feet. "Unless ghosts can stick tape on doors and put on rubber gloves. I'm going to email Dr. Moravec and see what he has to say."

CHAPTER 14

# THE VOICE OF THE RAVEN

Once she'd sent the photos and a detailed text to her grandfather she breakfasted on cereal and milk in the pleasant silences of the kitchen, and took a moment to sprinkle pepper out of the pepper shaker into her shoes. As she was finishing the cereal, Jill came in. "I hope you're feeling up for another ride. Corazon's looking happier than I've seen her in weeks. She likes the exercise." She shrugged. "And I think it would do us both some good to get out of here for a little while."

That succeeded in chasing off some of Ariel's mood, and she said something agreeable and went upstairs to change into jeans. By the time they got out to the barn Ricky had already finished tending the horses and left for the day, but the cool shadows inside the barn were pleasant enough, and Ariel followed Jill over to the beam that supported the saddles.

Something was wrong. That was Ariel's first thought, the moment she picked up the saddle and hauled it over to the stalls, and the thought stayed with her until she set the saddle down and went back to get the rest of the tack. She could feel it again, faint but inescapable, as she crossed the barn again and came close to the saddle. Some other morning she might have ignored the feeling, but the text from her mother and the bitter memories it brought had left her nerves feeling raw, and the other thing that had happened, the sound and the unseen presence, would not leave her thoughts. She gave the girth and the other fittings a close look to make sure nothing was dangerously worn, frowned, and turned the saddle over.

On the underside, right up beneath where she would sit, was a little packet of red cloth, handstitched and held in place by a piece of tape. Ariel reached for it and jerked her hand back, feeling the wrongness concentrated there. She turned to Jill. "Do you know what that is?"

Jill glanced over, did a double take, and said, "No. No, I don't, and there shouldn't be anything there."

Ariel already had her cell phone out by then, and snapped three pictures of the thing. A flurry of thumb strokes explained what had happened, and the text and the photos went off to her grandfather. "Give me a minute," she said then, and headed back to the farmhouse at a trot.

"Forgot something," she said to Ben's startled glance as she went through the parlor. Up in her room, her suitcase disgorged one of the padded envelopes Dr. Moravec had given her: big and sturdy, with one-day express mail labels on the outside and the postage already paid. She came trotting back out just as quickly.

"That might have a spell in it," she said to Jill, "and Dr. Moravec wants anything like that as fast as possible. Is it okay if we ride down to where the old mansion was, and you take the horses from there while I go on into Criswell? I can walk back and then help with the horses once we both get here."

"Sure, we can do that," said Jill, looking flustered.

It took Ariel a little fumbling with an old screwdriver to pry the packet of red cloth loose without touching it and pop it into the envelope, but she managed it, and sealed the envelope. "There. Now we can have a nice pleasant ride."

Corazon submitted patiently to Ariel's slightly uncertain ministrations and, saddled and bridled, followed her out into the yard. Jill and Stormalong were already there, and Ariel clambered a little awkwardly into the saddle with the envelope tucked under one arm. From there the four of them retraced the route of the morning before, out through the pasture to the old lane, and then at a gallop down the lane toward Criswell. The day was bright and clear, and the last traces of the morning's freshness still lingered in the lane, but Ariel barely noticed. Every scrap of her attention that wasn't focused on staying in the saddle and clinging to the envelope was circling around the simple question of why the amulet, if that was what it was, had shown up when and where it had.

It hadn't been there the morning before, she was certain of that. Had it been there that afternoon, when she'd helped Ricky with the horses? Maybe, Ariel thought, but it didn't seem likely: she'd been close to the same saddle and felt nothing amiss, nothing like the sense of wrongness that had grated on her nerves in the morning. Overnight, then. The same person who'd gone down into the basement and made off with the talismans, the same person who'd sent the unseen thing after her, had left another calling card. What it would have done, Ariel didn't know, but she could guess: horses were skittish at the best of times, and even a well-trained horse might be goaded somehow into bucking and flinging a rider off its back.

Having the amulet in the envelope didn't seem to trouble Corazon any, fortunately, and Ariel wondered whether her grandfather had put something protective in the padding. After a good brisk gallop down the lane, she drew rein by the ruins of the old mansion, where Jill and Stormalong were waiting. She swung down from the saddle, handed the reins to Jill, and said, "Thank you. Seriously, thank you. It's been way too long since I've been riding."

"Tomorrow, maybe," said Jill, with a smile that looked as though it took an effort.

"Maybe," said Ariel, smiling in response. "I'll have to see what Dr. Moravec wants."

Clippety-clop of the horses' hooves sounded behind her, fading slowly, as she headed east on the half-familiar dirt road. The old colonial cemetery drowsed in the morning sunlight, and the ribbons on the thorn tree above Hepzibah Rewell's grave hung limp in the still air. As she walked on past, Ariel brooded over the things she'd seen and heard at the Kellinger farm. It all fit together in a single pattern, she was sure of that, but what the pattern was still eluded her.

The thing she'd found under the saddle, that was an important piece of the pattern. It occurred to her suddenly that someone must have known she would be riding that morning. That narrowed the field a little, but only a little. June Northam had been watching the morning before, and could have guessed; Dot Kellinger could easily have seen her from the windows of her house; Jill and Ben knew, of course, and so did Olive, and—

A sudden memory struck her as she walked. Suzanne knew. She'd mentioned it to Suzanne, without thinking, as they'd walked back up the dirt road toward the Kellinger farm. Ariel considered that, and winced, telling herself to be more careful.

Criswell itself showed no more signs of life than it had the afternoon before. The businesses drowsed in the sunlight, the cartoon bull on the sign over Eddie's Burgers grinned vacuously, and the sound of a distant tractor emphasized the stillness. Another noise joined it as Ariel started along the sidewalk: a bus from Adocentyn with 38 VIA ELMHURST TO CRISWELL on the route sign came rumbling up Lafayette Road and stopped at the bus stop. Nobody got off and nobody boarded. The driver, half visible through the windshield, sat back and got out a thermos: the end of the line, Ariel guessed, and a few minutes of break time before the bus went back the way it had come.

For all she could tell, she thought in a burst of bleak emotion, everyone behind those faded lace curtains and clapboard-covered walls knew exactly what was happening to Jill and Ben, knew who had put the amulet under the saddle, and who was behind it all. If they did, they wouldn't breathe one word of that knowledge to city folk, much less to an eighteen year old from the other side of the state who happened to come blundering into the middle of it all. Was she simply wasting her time there? That seemed likely enough, and the thought came surging up that she could just toss the envelope and the amulet in the nearest trash can and walk away from it all. She clenched her jaw and kept going.

After the glare outside, the post office lobby seemed dim and sephulchral. Two people already stood in line waiting for the clerk, who was busy dealing with an old man's complicated question about a registered letter. Ariel got in line, feeling bored and uneasy. After a moment she glanced around. Framed black and white photos from a century back punctuated the beige plaster of the walls. Closest to her was an old map surrounded by a cheap wooden frame decades old and covered with glass that hadn't been washed in nearly as long. The heading at the top in ornate script read CRISWELL TOWNSHIP. Below that, a scale of miles, and the publisher's name, was the date, 1921.

Lacking anything better to do, Ariel considered the map. Despite the dust on the glass, Criswell itself was easy to find. To judge by the black shapes the map showed, the buildings hadn't changed much in a century. From the village she traced Lafayette Road east toward Adocentyn and then back west toward Norton Hill, and spotted the Kellinger acreage promptly enough, with the familiar narrow rectangle of the Witch's Wood framed by acreage to north, east, and west, and the little blue oval of Hoban's Pond near the middle of it. Then she traced the old dirt lane from the pasture past the northern edge of the woodlot to the black rectangle marking the Kellinger mansion, still standing then, and past it to the old cemetery and back to Criswell itself. All of it looked familiar enough, but her gaze kept returning to the map, until finally she realized what it was trying to tell her.

By then the man at the window had finished fussing over the registered letter. The other two customers had less complicated things to do, though they gave Ariel time to study one of the framed photos on the wall, a big Federal-era house with rowan trees around it that had to be the Kellinger mansion. Getting the amulet on its way to her grandfather took only a few moments once she got to the window, since the envelope was prepaid, and she brightened when the clerk told her that express mail hadn't gone out yet and it would get to the addressee with the afternoon delivery that same day. With that encouragement, she left the post office and started back toward the Kellinger farm.

She'd meant to walk back along Lafayette Road, but her mind was full of what the map implied, and before she'd quite realized what she was doing, she was walking up the narrow track between the fire station and the church. She shrugged, turned onto the old dirt lane, and kept going. The old cemetery was even more silent than before, without even a whisper of breeze to stir the ribbons on the thorn tree. She walked on past.

She was almost to the ruins of the Kellinger mansion when a black shape came winging up from the south and perched on the fence beside the lane. Ariel slowed, considering it: the same raven she'd seen before, she was sure of it. It tilted its head, observing her, then let out a harsh croak. A flurry of wingbeats took it a dozen yards or so further west, where it perched on the fence again.

Ariel kept walking. Every time she got close to the bird, it flew further along the road and sat there on the fence, watching her with one beady black eye as though waiting for her to catch up. The third time she got close to it she considered saying something to it, felt a sudden burst of embarrassment for having so ridiculous a thought, and then caught herself. It wasn't ridiculous at all, not when the Kellinger farm was entangled in witchcraft and only Aunt Clarice's toby had protected her from a creature in the night.

She'd lost count of the number of times the raven had flown ahead and waited for her by the time the Witch's Wood loomed up on the right. There, where Suzanne had clambered over the sagging fence boards, it perched one more time and let out a different cry, equally harsh but higher-pitched, demanding. Ariel slowed and stopped. The raven made the same noise again, and then jerked its beak toward the woodlot in a sudden imperious motion.

It wants me to follow. That was the first thought that passed through her mind, and the last one, too, once she'd circled through a dozen other baffled interpretations. She could think of at least a dozen good reasons why following it was the last thing she should do, and her grandfather's admonition to avoid taking risks was at the front of the pack, but none of them seemed convincing just then.

A sudden thought sent one hand into her purse, found the silver dime she'd gotten from Aunt Clarice. As she grasped it between thumb and forefinger, the raven ruffled its feathers as though startled, tilted its head to look at her from a different angle, and then gestured again with its bill toward the woodlot.

Ariel tried to convince herself that she should ignore it, and failed. A moment later she was clambering over the fence. The raven let out a croak that sounded vaguely satisfied, and flew to a low tree branch a dozen yards ahead, along the narrow trail that led alongside the woodlot toward Lafayette Road. It watched her from there. She considered it for a moment and finally said, "Where are you leading me?"

It made another harsh croaking cry. Wordless, it still communicated urgency: something important, and close by. Ariel nodded, as though the bird could understand her, and said, "Okay." The raven tilted its head, and waited until she'd started along the trail, then flew further on and waited for her from another branch.

She followed it halfway to the road before it let out another cry, and flew a few yards deeper into the woodlot. Ariel stopped, gathered up as much courage as she could find, and went after it. There was no trail, but the gaps between the trees were wide enough that she had no trouble making her way. Once she'd gotten past a few sparse shrubs at the woodlot's edge, no undergrowth hindered her. Dry pine needles turning slowly back to dirt cushioned her steps, filled the space beneath the trees with a silence that was almost palpable.

She didn't have to go far. She was barely out of sight of the cornfields and the path before she reached Hoban's Pond, and understood why the raven had brought her there.

The pond itself was maybe twenty yards across, a near-circle full of still water that reflected the hard blue of the summer sky. The pines grew close to the water most of the way around the pond. Over to Ariel's right, splashed with sunlight, was a narrow clearing with what looked like the traces of a small building's foundation, and the remains of an old fireplace and chimney made of river-rounded stones.

Prompted by the raven, who flew that way and called to her in an agitated tone, she picked her way around the pond. It had to be the site of Hepzibah Rewell's cabin, she was sure of it. Once she got close enough to see what was in the middle of the old foundation, though, that thought went somewhere else in a hurry.

The first thing she spotted was the traces of a fire in the old fireplace: a few blackened sticks and a little heap of ashes that looked fresh. Then she saw the red things around the inside of the foundation. There were five of them, making a rough circle. Once Ariel got close enough, she could see that they were the stubs of candles. Like the ashes, they didn't look as though they'd been out in the weather long.

The raven, perched on a branch of a nearby pine, croaked a sharp warning call at her before she got much closer. She'd already stopped, sensing something in and around the candles that made her skin crawl. Instead of approaching the place, she got out her phone, woke the camera, and started snapping pictures: the whole scene, the sticks and ashes in the old fireplace, the candles. She was moving the view of the lens from one candle to another when she caught sight of something small and pale in the middle, and zoomed in further. The pale thing was a bone with red threads tied around it, and it rested on a scrap of something mottled that Ariel couldn't identify at first.

She took one photo, another, zoomed in further, then studied the image on the screen and recognized the mottled shape. It was a piece of paper that had been set on fire, and all of it had burned black except for one corner, which was ordinary paper-white with a tiny spot of yellow.

A moment passed, and another, as that sank in. Ariel looked up at the raven. It croaked at her in a way that rang with finality, spread its wings, and flew off without looking back. Ariel panicked briefly, trying to figure out how to find her way back out of the woodlot without being seen by anybody, but something she'd learned at summer camp came to her rescue. Even under the pines she could see the sun clearly enough. She backed away from the ruins of the witch's cabin, then turned so the sun was off past her right shoulder, and kept it there while she picked her way back through the pines.

A few minutes later she reached the trail, drew in a long ragged breath, made sure her phone had a signal, and sent a text to her grandfather telling him what had happened and what she'd seen. She followed that with the pictures, then put the phone away, steadied her nerves with another deep uneven breath, and headed back toward the dirt lane.

She'd just finished letting herself into the pasture and closing the gate behind her when the phone chimed. She got it out of her purse. A glance at the screen showed her grandfather's number, so she picked up. "Hi."

"I asked you not to take risks," he said.

"This one wasn't my idea."

"It was still far more dangerous than you have any way of knowing. I'm on my way. Please have your suitcase packed when I get there."

Aghast, Ariel opened her mouth to protest, and then shut it, knowing that she would be wasting her breath. "Okay," she said.

"Thank you. I'll be there in thirty minutes." He cut the connection. Ariel gave the phone a bleak look, clenched her eyes shut to keep tears at bay, then started walking toward the barn, feeling miserable and useless.

# CHAPTER 15

# A DOOR IN THE DISTANCE

"I shouldn't have brought you into this situation at all," Dr. Moravec said as the Buick pulled out onto Lafayette Road. He was in the driver's seat, his fingers closed on the wheel like an eagle's talons on its prey. "But that was my fault, not yours, and those pictures brought me to my senses. I wonder if you have any idea what you found."

Ariel sat huddled in the passenger seat, trying not to look at anything. After a moment, when she realized he expected a response, she said, "I think someone did evil magic there."

"Good. That's quite correct: evil magic of an unusually powerful and unpleasant sort. I'm fairly sure I know who did it, but at this point there's a test I can do that will settle the matter once and for all. I need to make certain preparations, and I also need the amulet you mailed to me. Thank you for that, by the way." With a little shrug: "Spotting that and mailing it wasn't the only useful thing you did, but it was the one that will probably matter the most."

Fields went past for a time as she thought about that. Finally: "I'm sorry if following the raven messed things up for you."

"No, not at all."

She sent an uncertain look his way, considered saying something, decided against it. Criswell came into sight. The Buick slowed as it went past the cluster of buildings, picked up speed

141

on the far side. Only then did Dr. Moravec go on. "But you must admit it would be awkward if I had to call your parents and have them come pick up a corpse."

That last word hung in the air between them, freighting it with old bitter memories, as the road slid past. "So people can do that with magic," she ventured.

"Under some circumstances, yes." He drove in silence for a while. "Magic is subtle. Did you know the Pentagon did studies to see if they could harness magic for military purposes?"

"Wasn't there a movie about that?"

"There was indeed. I knew some of the people who worked in the actual studies. They said the Pentagon dropped the project because magic didn't do what they wanted it to do. It's subtle, as I said. But—" He glanced at her, then turned his attention back to the road. "Some causes of death are just as subtle."

Ariel took that in. It occurred to her, as the fields rolled by, that her grandfather hadn't criticized her, much less berated her the way her mother would have done. Maybe, she thought, maybe he really does mean it. Maybe he was just worried about me. And that means—

She gathered all her courage together and said, "I know it's dangerous. But it feels like there's still something I have to do."

The old man gave her another quick glance, and then an unwilling nod. "That's the damnable thing about it."

It wasn't quite the last response she'd expected, but it was close. More of Lafayette Road slid past, and the first of the suburban tract housing came in sight ahead, before she knew what she had to say in response. "Maybe," she started, and had to force herself to go on. "Maybe I could ask Aunt Clarice to do a reading for me, to let me know what I should do."

Still another quick glance, even more impenetrable than usual, came her way. He said nothing. The last of the fields gave way to houses and yards, then to the strip malls lining the Old Federal Pike. The Buick slowed to a halt, glided into motion again as the traffic gapped open. The towers of Adocentyn rose in the middle distance, looking pale and spectral in the gathering summer haze.

"Yes," he said finally. "Yes, I think that's probably the wisest choice."

Ariel closed her eyes and sent a silent thank you to nobody she could name. Maybe, she thought, maybe wishes sometimes do come true. She let another block go past. Then, tentatively: "Is it okay if I ask about the evil magic?"

That got her a long silence, and then a nod. "There's a root," the old man said. "I trust you won't mind if I don't mention which one. Harvested at the right time and treated in the right way, there are certain very helpful things you can do with it. There's also a wrong time and a wrong way. Do that and you can obtain a particularly unpleasant kind of familiar spirit. It has to be fed with drops of your blood, but in exchange it can do certain things for you. It can haunt people, harm them, steal their life energy and bring it to you."

"The thing that I felt last night."

"Exactly. I knew from what Ben and Jill told us earlier that there was a wraith involved—that's the proper term for the sort of spirit you had to deal with—but there are wraiths and then there are wraiths. The photos you sent me made it clear that we're dealing with one of the more dangerous kinds; that ritual isn't necessary otherwise. But there's another point."

Ariel glanced at him.

"Anyone who could do that ritual can recognize the talismans that I put in the basement," he said, "and know how they were made. Whoever sent the wraith knows that Ben and Jill have brought in a mage, and that means their chances of surviving until sunrise tomorrow aren't good unless I act." He shrugged. "So one way or another I'll be returning to the farm later today, to end this once and for all."

He said nothing else until the Buick pulled up alongside the familiar green house. "Well." He opened his door, turned to her. "I'll see if Clarice is available, and then—" One of his fractional shrugs punctuated the sentence.

Ariel got her suitcase from the back seat and followed him into the house. By the time she was climbing the stair she could hear her grandfather's precise voice, talking on the phone. From the foot of the bed, Nicodemus the wolf greeted her as enthusiastically as a stuffed animal can, his blind gaze fixed on her as she came through the door and his tongue lolling out, and she scruffed the fur on his head as she passed by to set the suitcase down by the closet.

Dr. Moravec was already off the phone when she came back downstairs. "I'm glad to say Clarice is having a quiet day," he said. "I'd recommend that you go as soon as you're ready."

"I can go now," said Ariel, feeling another rush of relief as a second obstacle cleared itself out of the way. Then, because it had to be said: "I can have her call you once I leave and tell you what the reading said."

"That won't be necessary," he replied at once. "I'll trust you to tell me what she says."

Ariel's gaze jerked up to his face. She swallowed. "Thank you."

He nodded, and she went past him to the door.

On the way down to Aunt Clarice's shop, she tried to think about what her grandfather had said about the evil magic, the root harvested and treated in the wrong way, the wraith she'd heard and felt stalking through the farmhouse in the night, the ritual that commanded it. Her mind would not stay on those topics. It kept circling back to the map she'd seen in the post office and the scrap of paper she'd spotted in the place by Hoban's Pond where Goody Rewell had lived all those years ago.

It all reminded her of one of the word search puzzles she'd found now and again in magazines, the kind where words would be hidden in among a grid of meaningless letters. Sometimes she'd had to go methodically through the grid, line by line and column by column, forward and backward, but sometimes she'd suddenly catch sight of the first and last letters of some elusive word, and a glance would be enough to tell her what the word was. The map was the first letter and the scrap of paper was the last, and between them, one letter after another fell into place, filling in the name of the one who'd cast the spells on Jill and Ben—and on Ariel.

She wondered, as she neared Aunt Clarice's shop, if she ought to call her grandfather right away and tell him what she'd figured out. It took her most of a block to decide against it. He seemed confident enough in his own knowledge, and though Ariel was just as sure of her own insight she was less certain of how seriously the old man would take her.

Later, maybe, she thought as she reached the door of the shop. Later, when I find out what he knows—and how.

The neon signs still burnt in the windows of the shop, inviting her in, proclaiming Aunt Clarice's omniscience. Inside, the same cool comfortable dimness and the same gallimaufry of unfamiliar scents greeted her. She let the door swing shut and tried to decide if she should call out or simply head back through the shelves full of candles and charms to the table in back. Before she could choose, Aunt Clarice's voice made the point moot: "Good morning, Ariel. Why don't you come right on back."

Ariel wove her way through the shelves to the back of the store. The little old woman sat at the table as though she hadn't moved a muscle since Ariel's first visit.

"Hi," said Ariel. "I hope you don't mind doing another reading for me."

"Not a bit." Aunt Clarice waved her to a chair at the table. "Quite a little tangle you landed yourself in."

"Yeah." Ariel stared at the table, embarrassed.

"Now, don't you go blaming yourself. You did what you were supposed to do."

Ariel processed that, then asked, "Does it matter if I saw the raven you talked about the last time I was here?"

Aunt Clarice gestured with one thin finger. "Now don't go confusing yourself with symbols like that. A raven you see in tea leaves is one thing. A raven you see flying in the air is something else again, and the one doesn't mean the same thing as the other. The raven you saw, did it bring anything bad your way?"

"No," Ariel admitted.

"Well, there you are. Now let's see where things go from here." She got to her feet, made tea as before. All the while Ariel struggled to keep her mind on something other than the choice ahead of her. Wasn't that something you had to do when you were getting a reading?

"No," said Aunt Clarice, as though the words had been spoken aloud. Ariel looked up sharply, blushing. The old woman laughed, finished filling the teacup, and came back to the table. "Sure, it's a bit easier when you're a beginner if the client keeps a quiet mind," she told Ariel. "But it's been a couple of years since I started studying these things, you know." Ariel's blush deepened, and Aunt Clarice laughed again.

"Now," she said. "I don't need to see your past, I know enough of that from the last reading, and Bernard told me a few things first thing this morning, too, when he came by to get some herbs he doesn't keep on hand." She made a tisking noise back in her throat. "So I know you've landed in the middle of a fight between witches, three of them." Startled, Ariel looked up sharply at the old woman's face, but she was staring into the tea. "Two are living and one is dead, and one or the other of the living ones won't be alive much longer, no matter what happens. That kind of trouble happens more often than I'd like, and as often as not it draws in some poor soul who doesn't know the first thing about any of this business." Aunt Clarice glanced up from the tea. "Tell me this. Do you have pepper in your shoes, like I said?"

"Yeah. I put some in fresh this morning."

"Good. And the silver dime I gave you, do you still have that?"

By way of answer, Ariel got the dime out of her purse, put it on the palm of her hand, and held it out.

"Good. That has to be touching your skin to protect you. Make sure you have it close."

Ariel nodded.

"The other—well, you'll have to decide if you want to take things that far. Now let's see what the leaves have to say." Aunt Clarice swirled the tea in the cup, poured it out into the bowl as before, and set the cup on the saucer and slid them halfway across the table toward Ariel. Brown-black shapes dotted the white porcelain, hinting at meanings Ariel thought she could almost begin to guess.

"The first thing to look at is here." A knotted brown finger pointed at two streaks of tea dust, forming parallel lines. "That means a trip of some kind, but it also means a decision. You've got to make a choice, and nobody else can make it for you. Either way—" She glanced up at Ariel. "Your life won't be the same afterward."

The finger moved further down, to a long thin leaf with a little blob of leaves at one end. "The axe means judgment. It's not just you who's going to choose, and not just you who's going to change. Something's going to get settled once and for all. Look at the way the handle goes toward the side of the cup, not toward the handle but not away from it either. You might take it in hand and you might not.

"Now over here." Ariel followed the pointing finger further down, where two scraps of leaf formed a right angle. "A corner like this shows danger. You need to keep your wits about you, because there's something waiting around that corner that you don't know about. If you don't take care you could end up in real trouble. See these dots right next to the corner? Each of those tells you to pay attention. One dot means it's important, but a whole bunch of them mean you really have to keep your eyes wide.

"And then finally, down here." Aunt Clarice pointed to the bottom of the cup, where a scattering of leaf fragments almost formed a shape like a T, but with the lines not quite touching. "That's something that hasn't quite finished coming into your life. A turning point, a place where you can go some other way and do something new with yourself. See how the line starts near the handle? That's how you know it's you that the leaves mean. But that hasn't happened yet. It might, or it might not. It's like a door you see off a ways from you, and you might get to it but you're not there yet."

Ariel waited for a silent moment, but the old woman had finished. After another moment: "What I have to know is whether I should go back into—well, into the mess I was in. Into the fight between the witches."

Aunt Clarice glanced up at her again. "Nobody in this world can answer that but you. That's what the leaves say."

Ariel nodded. "Thank you. I—I should go back to Dr. Moravec's place."

The old woman made a shooing motion with one hand. "You get going, then. Come back sometime once you get the chance. I'll find out what happens as soon as it happens, but I've got a pretty good guess that you'll have some other questions by then." One wrinkled brown hand repeated the motion, and Ariel thanked her again and fled.

Once the door closed behind her, Ariel stopped for a moment, closed her eyes, drew in a deep breath, and braced herself. She had one more errand to run before she started back for her grandfather's house.

Five minutes later she left the hardware store next to Aunt Clarice's shop, a set expression on her face, and started back up the slope toward Culpeper Park. The day was pleasant, cooler than the days before and graced with big billowing white clouds sliding eastward across a vast blue sky, but Ariel scarcely noticed. All the way back to her grandfather's house she wondered if she would have the courage to do what she knew she needed to do, and whether Dr. Moravec would take the choice away from her after all.

He was waiting in the parlor when she came in, settled comfortably on a sofa, and glanced up from one of his big leatherbound books of magic.

"She told me I have to decide," Ariel said.

He said nothing, just watched her with the terrible calm she'd learned to trust.

"I want to go," she said. "I think there's something I'm supposed to do, and I'm pretty sure I know what it is."

He set the book aside, unfolded himself from the sofa. "Then we can go at once. The amulet got here maybe ten minutes after you left. It was quite an obnoxious piece of work. The person who made it wanted the horse to run wild and throw you off."

Ariel gave him a bleak look. "I wondered if it was something like that."

Dr. Moravec nodded, and then smiled. It was not a gentle smile. It was precise, almost surgically so, and cold. "Fortunately you saw it. Even more fortunately, I know what to do with it. Someone who makes an amulet like that puts some of their own power into it, and that means they can be summoned by means of it. Shall we?" He gestured back the way she'd come.

"I'm ready." She stepped out of the way, followed him out through the hall to the door, and from there to the Buick.

"I'll drive," he said as they reached the car. "I'll drop you off when we arrive. There are three things I need you to do."

"Okay." She climbed into the passenger seat, closed the door.

He got behind the wheel, pulled his door shut, and started the engine. As it settled down to a steady purr: "The first is to have someone get a fire burning in the fireplace. The second is to throw something into it, and make sure it lands in the middle of the flames. Can you do that?"

"Yeah."

"Excellent. The amulet's linked to the one who made it, as I said, and once it's burnt with certain herbs, which I happen to know quite well, the person in question will be forced to come to the fire. Once that person arrives, I want you to make sure that everyone stays in the farmhouse. Don't let anyone leave if there's any way you can prevent it. That's the third thing. Do that, and keep the fire going so something else can be thrown into it, and this whole business will be settled soon enough."

Ariel glanced at him, and wondered what he had in mind, but he said nothing more. The Buick pulled away from the curb, began weaving through the streets of Adocentyn, heading toward the Old Federal Pike.

## CHAPTER 16

# AN AVENGING ANGEL

"Ready?" Dr. Moravec asked.

Ariel forced a smile. "Yeah, I think so."

He pulled over onto the roadside where the Witch's Wood came closest to Lafayette Road and the pines blotted out the buildings of the Kellinger farm. Once the car rolled to a stop, he extracted something from his pocket and handed it to Ariel. She took it—a plump envelope of brown paper with something thick inside it—and climbed out of the Buick, closing the door behind her as quietly as she could. Once she moved away from the car, Dr. Moravec drove on, leaving her there by the Witch's Wood and the sagging white fence.

She gathered up her courage and walked to the driveway, then started up it. Her footfalls seemed unnervingly loud on the packed dirt. Overhead, big white clouds drifted by, and the heat of the day thickened around her.

When she reached the door, she stopped. One of the instructions Aunt Clarice had given her was on her mind, and she needed the silver dime in a place where a clumsy movement of a hand wouldn't lose it. A sudden thought told her what to do. It only took a moment for her to get the dime from its place in her purse and tuck it into one side of her bra, low down under the breast where its presence wouldn't be seen. The metal felt cold against her skin at first, colder than the temperature of the day would explain.

That last preparation made, she let herself into the farmhouse.

Jill was in the parlor with a book in her lap, looking haggard, and a clatter of dishes out in the kitchen let Ariel know where Ben was. The painter looked up suddenly from her book, then saw that it was Ariel and put on a smile she obviously didn't feel. "Hi, Ariel. Is your grandfather with you?"

"He'll be here in just a few minutes. He has to do something first."

"Okay. It's—it's been pretty bad."

"I know. Is it okay if I go get Ben?"

Jill turned in her seat. "Honey? Can you come here for a bit?"

Something indistinct sounded from the kitchen. A moment later Ben came in, drying his hands on his slacks. "Hi, Ariel. I hope you've brought some good news."

"I hope so. I know who's behind everything that's been happening." That got her sudden startled looks; she went on. "But there are a couple of things we need to do right away. First of all, you're both still wearing the amulets, right?" They nodded. "Okay, good." She turned to Ben. "Can you get a fire going in the fireplace here? My grandfather needs that."

"Sure thing." Ben got to work at the fireplace, setting a neat little stack of split pine branches and then lighting it. Jill watched with an uncertain expression. Ariel waited until the fire was going strong and Ben stood back. Then she approached it, took the envelope she'd been given, and tossed it neatly into the center of the burning branches.

The moment it hit, the flames changed from yellow to pallid blue. A sharp astringent smell spread through the parlor, faded out as the chimney began to draw. Ariel turned to find both of the others staring at her. "What was that?" Jill asked.

Ariel shrugged. "Something Dr. Moravec gave me. Now I need the two of you to stay here in the house. Someone's going to come—"

As if on cue, a knock sounded on the kitchen door. "Yes, you can get that," Ariel said at once. "Whoever it is, please invite them in. It's important."

Jill got up and went into the kitchen. The sounds of the door opening pushed their way past the crackle and hiss of the burning pine branches, fell back into silence. Voices sounded half-heard thereafter, and then Jill came back into the parlor. Behind her was Olive Kellinger.

Something had changed about the old woman, though it took Ariel a moment to realize what it was and guess why. The vivid sense of life and joy that had surrounded her was gone as though it had never existed. The face that turned toward her and Ben was haggard, with cold bleak eyes framed by hard lines. It was only then that Ariel knew for certain that she was right, that the pieces of the puzzle she'd fitted together meant what she thought. More than that: she knew that the silver dime had freed her from a spell.

"If you like," the old woman was saying. "I really can't stay long."

"Oh, hi, Mrs. Kellinger," Ariel said. "I'm glad you're here. Dr. Moravec's going to be here in a few minutes and he's found out something about the stuff that's been happening here."

It was the wrong thing to say, she realized that at once. Mrs. Kellinger's face tensed, and she said, "Why, that's very good to hear, but I really do need to get back—"

Forced to her last resource, Ariel interrupted her. "No, Mrs. Kellinger, you need to sit down and we all need to talk. This is important. This is really important."

The old woman regarded her for a moment, and then went to one of the chairs and sat down. "If you insist," she said. "Please go ahead."

Ariel's nerves nearly failed her then, but she drew in a deep breath. The mystery novels she'd read so avidly came to her aid then, reminding her how a detective was supposed to lay out the solution to a case. "It's really simple, Mrs. Kellinger. You need to tell us why you've been practicing witchcraft, and why you've been using it on Jill and Ben and me."

Mrs. Kellinger looked up at her, the movement sudden and sharp.

"Because you're the one who's been casting the spells. It wasn't the ghost of Hepzibah Rewell, it wasn't the Northams, it wasn't Bill or Dot Kellinger, and it wasn't Oscar Bremberg or Suzanne. It was you." Ariel raised one finger. "If it was someone else, someone who wanted to hurt you, things would have happened in the barn and spooked the horses. They didn't, because you can't afford to lose the income from the boarding fees. You can get new tenants from out of state, the way you got Jill and Ben, but you can't get people around here to board their horses with you that way."

"She had the same sort of problems we did," Jill protested.

"Did you see anything happen in her cottage?" Ariel asked her at once. To Ben: "Did you?" Before they could answer: "All we know is what you said, Mrs. Kellinger, and after you said that plate got broken, you gave me your trash and there wasn't a broken plate in it."

"You're lying," Mrs. Kellinger said then, in a voice gone suddenly harsh.

"No, and you know I'm not," said Ariel. She raised a second finger. "You grew up right around here, close to Criswell. You had to know about Goody Rewell's grave and the way that people tie ribbons on the thorn tree there. Everyone here knows about those. When we first met, though, you said that you didn't know where she was buried and hadn't heard of any custom people could use to get on her good side. I found out the truth about that the first time I went to Criswell. Maybe there's a good reason why you lied, but it really looks like you wanted to blame Goody Rewell for what you were doing."

She raised another finger. "You lied to me about the Witch's Wood, too. There's a map of the Criswell area in the old post office from 1921 and it shows the woodlot around Hoban's Pond the same size it is now. 1921 was seventeen years before the Kellinger mansion burned down, so it wasn't anything Jasper Kellinger did to the Witch's Wood that brought a curse down on him. As far as I can tell there wasn't a curse at all. I looked up the Kellingers, and they haven't been especially rich or important since the 1850s. That's another way you were trying to blame Goody Rewell for something she didn't do."

By then Jill and Ben were staring at her, their faces aghast. She ignored them and went on, raising one more finger. "You're the only other person who's likely to have a key to the basement here, and somebody got down there last night to take away the talismans. Your glasses aren't good enough, by the way—you replaced the tape but you didn't notice that you used the wrong kind of tape or that I'd signed the piece I put there. You knew that I was going to ride Corazon this morning, and you had plenty of time last night to put an amulet under the saddle, which I found. And I also found the place by Hoban's Pond where Goody Rewell lived, and I saw what you left behind after you cast your latest spell there. I know it was you because you used a piece of paper in the spell, and it didn't all burn up. It's the same paper you use for notes, the kind with the little geese on top. Do you know how I found the place, Mrs. Kellinger? A raven led me there."

The old woman sucked in a sudden breath. "Foolish girl," she said, in the same harsh voice. "Foolish, foolish girl. Look at me."

"No." Ariel didn't have to force the smile. "And it wouldn't help you if I did."

Mrs. Kellinger stared at her for a moment, then turned toward Jill and Ben. Whatever she saw there gave her no comfort, and she sprang to her feet and scurried toward the door to the kitchen. Ben stood up and started after her.

Before either of them could reach the door, someone else stepped into sight through it. Suzanne, Ariel thought, and then blinked. Was it Suzanne? The black hair had turned strawberry blonde, the gray eyes had gone bright blue, and the long ugly scar had vanished, but the woman who stood there had the same height and build and the clothes were the same kind of plain farm gear Ariel had seen Suzanne wearing. In her hand she had a steel awl with a wooden handle, the point polished and bright.

Mrs. Kellinger staggered back as though she'd hit a wall. "*You!*"

"Hi, Olive," said the woman, a hard smile on her face, and it was Suzanne's voice. "Been a little while, hasn't it?" She took a step in from the door.

The old woman let out a little desperate cry, turned, and darted back the other way. Ariel was ready. She'd reached into her purse and brought out her hardware-store purchase, the largest steel nail they'd had in stock, half the length of Suzanne's awl but nearly as sharp. It glinted in her hand as she moved to block the way to the entry and the front door.

Mrs. Kellinger stopped and then darted forward, snatching at Ariel's hands. Ariel twisted out of the way and slashed reflexively with the nail. The old woman jerked back out of range just in time. She stared at Ariel with narrowed eyes. Her breath came fast and quick.

"Don't make me use this," said Ariel. "Please don't make me use this."

Mrs. Kellinger laughed, a high shrill laugh that set Ariel's teeth on edge. "No, no, of course not. Not that, not anything else ever again." She stepped back into a corner of the room and stretched out a hand toward Ariel, fingers spread. Her voice rose, shrill and shaking: "*Thebot, Wethor, Yrwote, Yrzon! Coniuro vos, spiritus acherontici—*"

From the moment she spoke the first word, the air in the room turned cold and somehow slippery, and the lights dimmed. Ariel found herself fighting a sudden creeping numbness. Time stretched into slow motion. Each word the witch uttered seemed to take longer than the last, while off beyond her, Suzanne came closer with terrible slowness. Ariel gathered all her strength to lunge at the witch, but the air congealed—

"That's quite enough of that," said Dr. Moravec behind her.

Mrs. Kellinger looked past Ariel, startled, and the blood drained from her face. The cold slippery quality in the air faltered.

"I'm quite sure you know what this is and what it can do," Dr. Moravec went on. "Speak one more word of that spell or try to cast anything else, and I'll use it. Sit down with your hands in plain sight. Now!"

The cold slippery feeling faded away. Ariel shook off the effects of the spell and half turned, keeping Mrs. Kellinger in sight. Dr. Moravec stood just inside the door to the entry. In his hand, pointing at the old woman, was an object Ariel hadn't seen before: a trident of sorts, as long as the old man's forearm, with a handle of some black glossy substance and a head of flat gray steel marked with strange symbols and letters. Its three points glittered in a way the light inside the parlor didn't quite explain.

Mrs. Kellinger backed up and perched on the chair where she'd been sitting, though she stayed taut, like a beast ready to spring. No one else moved. Dr. Moravec spared a quick glance at the fireplace, then moved that way, keeping the trident pointed at the witch. "I would have preferred a less sudden and final way of settling this, Mrs. Kellinger, but you haven't given me that choice. For what it's worth, I'm sorry."

He reached the fireplace, took something out of his jacket pocket, and threw it into the heart of the flames. The fire flared up suddenly around it, pallid blue.

Mrs. Kellinger flung herself out of the chair with a shrieked *"No!"* The word ended in a sudden choking gurgle, and she toppled back into the chair, then rolled out of it and tumbled to the floor. Ben was on his feet an instant later, but paused long enough to send a questioning glance to Dr. Moravec, who gestured his assent.

"She's still got a pulse," Ben said a moment later, straightening. "And she's breathing." Ariel had to make an effort to believe him, for the old woman's face was gray and slack. A thin bluish smoke spread through the room from the fireplace. With it came an unpleasant smell, part acrid herbs, part burnt blood.

"That's too bad," said Suzanne. She'd put the awl away, but stood there just inside the kitchen door with the face of an avenging angel, harsh and exultant.

Dr. Moravec left the parlor for the entry, came back a moment later with his valise in one hand and the trident nowhere in sight. "If someone could call 911," he said, "that would be best. Tell them she seems to have suffered a stroke." Jill nodded, and left the room without a word. Ben got a cushion from the couch and put it under the old woman's feet.

"Just let her die," Suzanne said. "It'll be better for everyone."

"That will happen soon enough," Dr. Moravec told her.

"Excuse me," said Ben, looking at the newcomer. "You want to tell me who you are?"

Suzanne grinned. "Without the wig, the contacts, and the fake scar? She could have told you. You know me as Suzanne, but my full name's Josephine Suzanne Kellinger. I'm Glen Kellinger's daughter."

"The stepdaughter who ran away," Ariel said.

"So you knew about that? Good. Yeah, that's me."

Jill came back into the parlor. "The paramedics are on their way," she said. "They said it would take them five minutes, maybe." She looked at Mrs. Kellinger's limp form, shuddered, and then went to her husband and buried her face in his shoulder, shaking, while he held her.

A silence passed. The blue smoke cleared and the stench from the fireplace faded. "That was the blasting trident of Paracelsus, wasn't it?" Suzanne asked Dr. Moravec. "I've read of those but I've never seen one."

"Yes. You know quite a bit about these things, then."

"I spent twenty years in Memphis studying them."

The old man nodded.

After another long moment Jill straightened and went back to sit on the sofa, though she avoided looking at Mrs. Kellinger. Ben checked on the old woman again, and then went to join his wife on the sofa.

Dr. Moravec said, "I trust everyone's aware by now that she was responsible for everything that was happening here."

"Ariel told us," said Ben.

The old man sent a glance toward his granddaughter with as close to an expression of surprise as she'd ever seen on his face. He followed it with a nod, and turned to Ben and the others: "Once the paramedics have gone I can go into the details." To Suzanne: "I imagine you know quite a bit of those already, but maybe not quite all. It's rather an ugly story."

Faint at first, muffled by the window glass, the sound of a siren came through the still air.

## CHAPTER 17

# A WORD LEFT UNSPOKEN

"I'll have the hospital give you a call," one of the paramedics said to Ben. His face had the set look of someone who has no good news to offer. Ben and Jill both thanked him, and he hurried out of the parlor. The other two paramedics had left a moment earlier, steering a wheeled ambulance gurney with Olive Kellinger on it. They'd checked her vital signs, got oxygen hissing into her nostrils through a tube, and hooked her up to an IV, but her face stayed a sagging gray mask the whole time and no trace of consciousness showed in her empty eyes.

Ben went out after them, and Jill slumped back onto the sofa. After a moment Ariel found a place to sit, and so did her grandfather. Suzanne, who had stepped outside when the paramedics arrived, came back in and stood near the kitchen door. A minute passed, and then another. Nobody said anything.

The voices that finally broke the silence came from the entry. Ben appeared a little later with Dot Kellinger behind him. After her came a lean muscular man in jeans and a tee shirt, his face harsh and lined. "Jill, Ariel—" Ben started to say.

Dot looked past him as she came into the parlor and saw Suzanne. Her face blanched. "Oh my God," she said. "Josie."

Suzanne looked sheepish. "Hi, Aunt Dot. Hi, Uncle Bill. I go by Suzanne these days."

"Suzanne," the lean man said, considering her. "Damn. Not the one who's been staying at Bremberg's place? The one time I saw that Suzanne, she had black hair."

"That was me. You can do a lot with a wig and plenty of makeup—and I didn't want her to know I came back."

"But your face," said Dorothy. "You had an awful scar!"

Suzanne grinned. "It's from a theater supply. Let me sit you down sometime and get out my makeup box, and I promise you in half an hour you won't recognize yourself."

Dot nodded distractedly, and then went over to Suzanne and held out her arms tentatively. Suzanne hugged her and patted her back.

"This is Dot's husband Bill," said Ben, finishing the interrupted sentence. "Dr. Moravec? Bill and Dot Kellinger. They live right on the other side of the woodlot. Bill, this is Dr. Bernard Moravec and his assistant Ariel Moravec."

"Pleased to meet you," said Bill. "Hope we're not intruding. Heard the siren, and—" He shrugged, a quick expressive movement. "Thought somebody might need some help."

"Thank you," Jill said, standing up with an effort. She had recovered most of her composure by then, though she'd spent the whole time while the paramedics were there trying not to look at Mrs. Kellinger. "But I don't know if there's anything anyone can do. Olive collapsed—we're pretty sure she had a stroke."

Before anyone else could speak a knock came at the door. Ben went out and returned a moment later with Fred and June Northam, who'd just arrived on the same errand. Another round of introductions followed and then the half-truth had to be repeated again, an assortment of awkward condolences exchanged, hands shaken and promises of help spread around. The whole time, as she sat half curled up in a chair and said as little as she could, Ariel watched and listened. A word nobody spoke aloud hung in the air, cold and inescapable.

Witchcraft.

Did the Northams and the Kellingers know what Olive Kellinger had been doing? Ariel guessed they did, from the hints of nervousness whenever they mentioned her, the awkward signs of hope behind the conventional sentiments whenever anyone spoke of her condition or her likely fate. Ariel thought of Dot's hissed words when she'd mentioned witchcraft. Maybe, she thought, that kind of thing happens all the time in farm country. Maybe it happens just often enough that everyone knows about it. Maybe—

Guesses spun off into the unknowable as Dot gave Suzanne another hug and told her to come by as soon as she could. Bill shook her hand and said the same thing. After that the Northams and the Kellingers said their goodbyes, asked Ben and Jill to let them know as soon as any news arrived from the hospital, and left. Once the door had closed behind them all, Ben came back from the entry and said to nobody in particular. "Well. That's as much excitement as I want this month."

"I quite understand," said Dr. Moravec. "I think I can promise you a much quieter and more pleasant time from now on."

"I'm glad to hear that," said Jill. "I'd really like to know what just happened. Suzanne, if you can stay a little while, I think you had something to do with that, didn't you?"

"She did indeed," said Dr. Moravec. "You had more help than you knew, and so did I. Ms. Kellinger, perhaps you can tell us all a little bit about that."

"Sure." Suzanne turned to face Jill and Ben. "I'm sorry I couldn't introduce myself before now. I didn't dare take the chance that she'd see through the disguise and the spells and figure out who I was. But, yeah, I cast some spells to try to keep you safe."

"Thank you," said Jill.

Ben motioned Suzanne to a seat, and she took one. "You're welcome," she said. "I came back here to stop her. I was just about to try to do that once and for all when Dr. Moravec here beat me to it."

"An amusing scene, in a way," said Dr. Moravec. "The spell I worked on the amulet Ariel threw into the fire was meant to force the person who was making all the trouble to come here. I was all but certain that it was Mrs. Kellinger, and once she came out of the cottage and headed for the house I had no more doubts. My plan was to go into the cottage, find the thing that was the foundation of her power, bring it here and burn it. Then, just as I went toward the cottage, I surprised Suzanne going the same direction for the same reason."

"I knew I could only risk going into the cottage during daylight hours," said Suzanne. "I saw what she'd done by the pond and I knew she was getting ready to do something really bad, something that would kill people, and I decided it was time to stop her once and for all. So I came over and hid in the woods by the cottage this morning, and waited. It was a long wait, but finally she left, and I headed for the cottage door. So did Dr. Moravec. He saw me, too, which takes some doing when I don't want to be seen—that's one of the things I learned how to do in Memphis. I figured out right away that he knows more about this stuff than I do, so I went to the kitchen door to make sure she couldn't get back to the cottage even if she tried."

"And I found the thing I was looking for." The old man's face tautened. "I won't go into details. It wasn't hard to find, though she'd hid it as carefully as she could. Magic that strong and that evil is easy enough to sense. I found the book where she learned her lore, too."

Suzanne gave him a sudden startled look. "You got the book."

"It'll be on its way to the Heydonian Institution shortly. An interesting specimen in its own unpleasant way: a handwritten journal from the middle of the nineteenth century, probably the private spell collection of some local sorcerer. I promise you it will be quite safe, and kept out of the hands of anyone who might misuse it."

"That's fair," said Suzanne. "As long as it's locked up some-where, I'm glad."

"It would be interesting to know how she got it," said Dr. Moravec. "Though I don't imagine we'll ever know. It's not pleasant reading." To Jill and Ben: "The thing you heard and felt at night was a wraith—a type of familiar spirit. One of the things it could do was steal other people's life force and bring that back to its mistress. She was doing that to people in the area to keep herself healthy and strong."

"Like a vampire," Jill ventured.

"Very much like a vampire. That's why she kept bringing in new tenants, and why they kept getting sick and leaving. It's why so many people came down with illnesses in the farms close by here. That's also why once the two of you started say-ing the Cao Dai prayers to protect yourselves, she tried to drive you away, so she could get someone more vulnerable. That's not the only thing her familiar did, but it's the one that mat-tered most." He gestured, dismissing the other possibilities. "Once I burnt the amulet that housed her familiar spirit, all the life energy she'd had it steal for her went away at once. You saw the result."

"I wish it didn't have to be so—well, so sudden," Jill said then.

"If you knew how long she'd been doing this," said Suzanne, "you might not think that."

"You must have seen a lot of it," Ben said then.

Suzanne nodded. "Yeah. Too much of it. I can tell you the story if you want to hear it."

"I think all of us do," said Dr. Moravec.

She closed her eyes for a moment, then went on. "It's a long ugly story. The really short version is that as soon as Dad remar-ried, when I was fourteen, I started having what I thought were nightmares. Something would come into my bedroom at night and press down on me. Every time that happened I was sick for days afterwards, and I couldn't think. I just couldn't think clearly at all. I didn't want to believe it was her. I liked her at first, but I finally noticed that every time it happened, she was bright and cheerful and full of energy the next morning. I talked to Dad about it, and she found out about it somehow and turned Dad against me, the way she turned him against everyone in his family.

"So I talked to some kids I knew at high school, and they told me I needed to go to an old man named Ernie Cobson who lived out Gallatin Road. He had a reputation for knowing things. One of the kids knew him, and got an amulet from him, a little bag I kept in my school locker—I didn't dare bring it home, I figured she'd know I had it, but it kept my mind clear. Finally I skipped school one day and went to talk to him. I didn't have to tell him anything. He just looked at me and told me that someone was feeding on my life and I wouldn't live to see twenty-one if I didn't do something about it. He was right, too. She didn't want anyone to come between her and Dad—or between her and Dad's estate.

"But I had a way to get out. A girl who was a really good friend of mine moved to Memphis the year before with her family. I texted her and told her a little of what was going on, and she talked to her folks and they agreed to give me a place to stay for a little while. I just had to get away, without her finding out, because I knew she'd stop me if she could. Having to leave suddenly like that hurt, because I had a horse my father gave me and I had to leave her behind, but I didn't have any other choice.

"All I needed to do is get into town, and I had a way to do that, too. Oscar Bremberg and I knew each other, and he was kind of sweet on me, and so I went to him and he agreed to help me. I went to school the next day, just like normal, but I packed clothes in my bag instead of textbooks and school stuff, and right after school Oscar picked me up and gave me a ride to the Adocentyn bus station. I had just enough money for the tickets, but before he left me he handed me five twenties to make sure I had food and things.

"So that got me to Memphis, and my friend's family was really kind, they put me up and didn't even ask me to chip into the food budget until I had a job. I got some fake ID saying I was eighteen, worked tables for a while, then got into theater— I knew I'd have to be able to disguise myself if I ever came back. The thing that mattered more than that was that I found some people who could teach me how to do things with roots and candles and spells. Not to do the things she did." Her face tensed. "To stop her, to stop her witchcraft. I hoped all along that I could come back here someday and do that. I wanted to be able to do that in time to see Dad again, but—" She made a little helpless gesture. "It didn't work out that way.

"I wanted to let Aunt Dot and Uncle Bill know I was okay, but couldn't be sure who I could trust. The one person I was sure of was Oscar. I wrote to him every Christmas, and he wrote back and kept me posted on what was happening here. So when I was finally ready, when I knew what I had to know and was ready to face her, I wrote to him again and asked if I could stay with him for a while, and he was—really sweet about it."

Ariel, watching the sudden softening of her face, had no trouble guessing just how sweet he had been.

"So I took the bus back from Memphis and got to the Adocentyn station at three in the morning, and Oscar picked me up there and brought me back to his place. I brought the wig and the contacts and the fake scar with me—I got those from a theatrical supply place in Memphis—and I had everything else I needed but some red ribbon."

"I saw your ribbon on the tree," said Ariel.

Suzanne nodded again. "I got it from Chuck Glaser at the General Store, of course. I wouldn't go anywhere else. But I was getting ready to confront her when the two of you showed up." A slow smile creased her face. "Don't think I object. I know some things and I was ready to take the risk, but it would have been a fight. As it was, the expression on her face when she saw me in the doorway is something I'm going to treasure forever."

Dr. Moravec let a moment pass, and then said, "I trust Oscar didn't have to deal with too much of her witchcraft."

Suzanne shook her head. "No. He knew what was living across the road from him. He got some protections from old Ernie Cobson when he was still alive, and then I sent him some things as soon as I knew how to make them. I wish I could have sent some protections to Aunt Dot and Uncle Bill. I know they went through hell. I went over there one night as soon as I came back, and got a couple of amulets hidden away in their barn to take some of the curse off their poor cows. I'll finish the job in the next few days and see if I can bring them some good luck instead." To Jill and Ben: "I don't know what your plans are now that she's gone, but if you need anything of the kind, I'm available."

"Thank you," said Jill. "We might." She turned to face Dr. Moravec. "If that's okay. I know you may have your own plans."

"Some," said Dr. Moravec. "It's important that the cottage is free of the energies of her magic, and the place where Hepzibah Rewell lived will have to be cleansed as well." To Suzanne: "That's work for more than one person."

"You're on," said Suzanne. "I'm pretty sure you know quite a bit I don't, but I studied with some top-notch root doctors in Memphis."

"I'm glad to hear that," said Dr. Moravec. "We can schedule something soon."

"I hope you don't mind my bringing this up," Ben said then, "but do you happen to know who'll inherit this place once your stepmother dies? The reason I ask is that Jill and I have been thinking about making an offer on the house and barn, if that's an option."

Suzanne considered that. "It might be. Dad's will left it to her while she lived, and then when she dies half of it goes to me and half to Uncle Bill and Aunt Dot. If things haven't changed too much, the acreage is worth half and the house and barn and cottage is the other half. I'd offer Bill and Dot the acreage—the rent they'd get from the Northams would leave them in really good shape financially—and I'd be up for selling my share." Her face softened again. "I'll be settling down with Oscar. He had some things to say when I called him just now."

"Congratulations," Jill said, and Suzanne blushed and thanked her.

Ben turned to Dr. Moravec. "Do you think it would be better to tear the cottage down?"

"That won't be necessary. Once it's cleansed, however, someone should live there. If it stays empty too long the energies could return."

"Can I say something?" Ariel asked. Four faces turned toward her. "Maybe you could see if Ricky wants to move in there. Jill, you were saying you wanted to board more horses, and I know she'd be really happy to take care of them."

"Ricky?" Suzanne said. "Is that Ricky Higgins, the one who's kind of funny?" Ariel sent an unfriendly look her way, but Suzanne went on: "If you want my advice, hire her as fast as you can and give her whatever she asks for. Her dad's uncle was the same way—he couldn't even talk, he had to write words on a pad of paper he had in his pocket, but there's never been anyone in this county half as good with livestock as he was. Ask anybody local about Ralph Higgins and you'll hear some stories."

Jill and Ben glanced at each other; he made a little shrug, as if to say, sure, if you want. "I'll talk to her sometime soon," Jill said.

A brief silence passed, and then Dr. Moravec unfolded himself from his chair. "Well," he said. "I think that settles everything for the moment." He extracted a business card and handed it to Suzanne. "Please call me when you have time and we can arrange to cleanse the cottage." To Jill and Ben: "If anything else happens, please let me know."

A few goodbyes later, he and Ariel went through the front door. Outside, the heat of the day had begun to pass, and the clouds overhead were thickening, scenting the breeze with the first faint hint of rain. The two of them said nothing while they walked to the old black Buick. Ariel climbed in, waited while Dr. Moravec tucked his valise in back and then settled in behind the wheel. Once the doors were shut and the engine was settling into its rhythm, the old man said, "I'd be very interested to hear how you knew Olive Kellinger was behind all this."

"Sure," said Ariel. She explained about the map in the post office, the little yellow trace of the goose's beak on the spell paper, the other hints and clues that fell into place around them. The whole time Dr. Moravec regarded her with one of his most impenetrable looks, and when she was done he nodded and then got the car in motion.

"How did you know?" she asked as it started down the driveway.

"I didn't know for certain until she came in response to the summoning spell," he said. "But I sensed that first morning when we came out here that it was someone who lived very close. I have a friend who works in the county vital records office, and so it was easy enough to get the birth dates and times of the Kellingers, the Northams, and Oscar Bremberg, cast their horoscopes, and see if any of them had the sort of indications that you would expect in the birth chart of a witch. Olive Kellinger's chart had them in abundance. I was concerned at first because I couldn't get the birth data for Suzanne, but—" He shrugged. "I was prepared for that possibility too."

"The trident," Ariel said then. "The blasting trident of—" She stopped, trying to recall the name.

"Paracelsus," said Dr. Moravec. "Philippus Aureolus Theophrastus Bombastus Paracelsus von Hohenheim, if you want to be precise about his name."

She choked with laughter. "Okay," she said, still laughing. "I'll try to remember that. What would it have done to her?"

"At the very least it would have knocked her unconscious. Depending on how much of her life force was stolen from others, it could have killed her on the spot. The blasting trident disrupts magic. A dangerous tool, in some ways, but it's proven useful to me more than once."

Ariel opened her mouth to say something, and stopped. There on one of the fence posts where the driveway met the road was a big black raven. Dr. Moravec slowed, glanced at it, and then at Ariel. The raven spread its wings and flew off, and the Buick pulled out onto Lafayette Road and turned back toward Adocentyn.

## CHAPTER 18

# A GAP FOR SUNLIGHT

Two days later, the phone rang in the study of the big green house on Lyon Avenue. Dr. Moravec got up from his armchair and went to answer it. Ariel, curled up in a corner of the sofa in the parlor with morning sun spilling across her, tried to concentrate on the book in her lap, and failed miserably. From above, the little wooden crocodile looked down with its toothy grin. She tried to ignore it, too, and didn't succeed at that either.

It wasn't the fault of the book—or, for that matter, of the crocodile. She'd asked her grandfather the day before to lend her a book that would help her make sense of magic, and he'd gone into his study and come out a few minutes later with a big nineteenth-century volume, leather bound and printed on luscious cream-colored paper. She'd read maybe half of it, too, before the silence of the night and her drooping eyelids had convinced her that sleep was a better option just then.

No, the problem was that she'd blinked awake suddenly that morning with a thought so enticing that she lay there with Nicodemus's fur in her face for something like fifteen minutes. She hadn't dared move, for fear that anything she did might cause the thought to pop like a bubble. Finally she'd gotten up, put Nicodemus in his place of honor at the foot of the bed, and gone about her morning routine, hoping against hope that

171

the thought wouldn't turn out to be a passing fancy. When it stayed unshaken in her mind, a kind of giddy desperation seized her. She tried over and over again to come up with some reason why things couldn't work out the way she hoped, and every effort failed.

Even the inevitable texts from her parents failed to dispel the thought or the trembling exhilaration it brought her. Her mother's text was curt and measured and brittle, her father's just as short but despairing; she read them both, left them unanswered, and finished getting ready for the day. The sunlight that splashed on the floor of the kitchen as she busied herself with breakfast seemed impossibly brilliant, as though she was walking on surfaces of pure light.

Something would have to be said. She knew that, and from what she'd learned of her grandfather's ways, it would have to be said at the right moment. So far that morning, the right moment had been annoyingly slow about putting in an appearance. As the deep murmur of her grandfather's voice came back from the kitchen in short bursts, Ariel made another attempt to lose herself in the book on magic. The effort didn't accomplish much. It didn't help that the phone conversation went on just at the edge of her hearing, so that she couldn't quite make out what Dr. Moravec was saying, and had no way to guess what was being communicated in the long moments when he listened in silence.

Just as she realized she'd read the same paragraph four times and still had no idea what it was talking about, sounds told of the phone returning to its cradle and Dr. Moravec leaving his study. Ariel looked up as he came back into the parlor.

"Well," he said. "That was Jill Callahan, with news. If you're not too busy—"

Ariel set the book aside. "No, not at all."

The old man settled into his armchair. "Things seem to be going satisfactorily, for everyone but Olive Kellinger. She died in the hospital late last night. I've advised them to see to it that she's cremated and her ashes scattered over running water." With a fractional shrug: "I wish there had been another way to stop her, but I don't know of one."

"I wonder why she did all that stuff," Ariel said.

"A reasonable question which I can't answer. If I had to guess, though, she probably stumbled into it a little at a time. Most people who practice evil magic do. They learn how to do the kind of small magic that can be used for good or evil, and it turns out that they end up using it to hurt more often than to help and heal. There are always reasons: old grudges and new ones, genuine mistreatment by other people, hopes and dreams that would be in reach if only something bad happened to someone else—" He shook his head. "To judge by what Suzanne Kellinger said, she was a competent and thoroughly evil witch before she married Earl Kellinger, and she was already using the wraith to take life energy from other people. But I don't imagine we'll ever know what got her started down that path."

Ariel nodded, and he went on. "At any rate, our clients contacted the Kellinger family lawyer, and she confirmed everything Suzanne Kellinger said. There's probate to go through, but the other Kellingers are happy to take the acreage as their half of the estate, and the Northams are just as happy to rent from them instead of their former landlady."

"That ought to make things a lot easier for Dot and Bill," said Ariel.

"So I gather. Jill mentioned that Dot was wiping tears from her eyes the whole time, out of simple relief. Partly having their financial problems solved, partly—" He gestured, palms up. "I'm quite sure they knew what Olive Kellinger was doing."

Ariel nodded again.

"Aside from that, Suzanne Kellinger has agreed to sell the house, the barn, and the horse pasture to our clients once the will has cleared probate. Jill mentioned that she talked to the young lady who takes care of the horses—"

"Ricky."

"Yes. Once she knew that Olive Kellinger was dead, she was delighted at the thought of moving into the cottage once it's available, and working full time for our clients as stable manager. If I understand correctly, there are twenty stalls in the barn, and Jill believes she can fill them all."

"Ricky'll be in seventh heaven if she does," said Ariel.

"Jill also mentioned that she hopes you can find time on weekdays now and then to come out to the farm and help give the horses a little exercise. She apparently finds you congenial company, and so does one of the horses. I'm sorry to say I don't recall the name."

The thought that she'd made a friend in Jill Callahan was unexpected enough that Ariel had to stop and gather her thoughts. "Corazon," she said. "I'll give her a call and tell her I'd love to come out there." A gesture pushed aside immense uncertainties. "While I'm still here."

"Yes, there is that." A moment passed, and another, as the old man considered her.

"I hope you won't take this amiss," he said finally, "but I was—" He paused, as though considering words. "Uncertain, shall we say, when your trip out here was decided on, about how well we'd get along. It's been a very long time since I've shared a home with another person: since your grandmother divorced me, in fact. But you've been remarkably easy to get along with, and you can handle the quiet I prefer, which is not that common. And of course your help with this latest case—" Another shrug. "Was really quite significant."

"Thank you," she said.

"You found a great deal of information very quickly, and handled a couple of difficult situations quite well, all things considered. All of which is to say that I'll feel a definite sense of regret when you go back to Summerfield."

It was the moment Ariel had been waiting for, she knew it in her bones. She gathered up all her courage and said, "I don't have to go back, you know."

That got her a sudden glance she couldn't read at all.

She made herself go on. "Mom and Dad told me I have to get a job or go to community college. Working as your assistant—that would be getting a job, right? And—" She shrugged, as though it didn't matter much, though it mattered more than anything else she could have named just then. "I really like being here." With a quick smile: "Seriously, it's the cat's meow. It's quiet, like you said, and you've been really nice. And I think I want to know more about magic. I don't know how much more, but more."

The silence that followed came as no surprise. She waited with as much patience as she could muster. "I couldn't afford to offer you a large salary," he said finally.

That was when Ariel knew she'd won. She managed to keep from whooping in sheer delight, settled for a luminous smile. "That's okay," she said. "Especially if the job comes with room and board."

He considered that, nodded once. "Yes. I think that would work very well."

She got to her feet, extended a hand. "Deal?"

Dr. Moravec rose also, and shook it. "Deal." They both sat down, and he went on: "I'll have to ask you to handle telling your parents. I don't think they'll take it well at all coming from me. I'm not sure how well they'll take it no matter who tells them, but—" A dismissive gesture finished the sentence. "You're eighteen and free to make your own choices, after all."

"No problem," said Ariel. "I already know what I'm going to tell them."

She didn't text them until the next day, though. A message to someone else came first, and that involved travel. She considered asking if she could borrow the Buick, but that felt a little like cheating. It felt instead as though she had to get there her own way, and that meant walking downtown to the transit mall, waiting there until the number 38 bus rolled up, climbing aboard and paying her fare and watching the scenery roll past as the bus wound its way through half a dozen suburbs and as many old farm villages to Criswell. The half-familiar buildings dozed in the afternoon heat the way they'd done those other times she'd been there, but this time she knew already where to go and what question to ask.

The old man behind the counter at the general store glanced up with the same practiced smile he'd aimed at her before, and listened to her question with a hint of amusement, as though he'd heard the same thing asked any number of times before. "Why, yes," he said when she'd finished. "And it's wise to say thank you, too, especially if you might need her help again. That's what I always heard, at least."

Ariel nodded and waited.

"It's quite a simple thing. She likes flowers on her grave. White flowers. Most people use the artificial kind, since they last longer. If you're interested—" He reached under the counter and pulled out a little bunch of white flowers tied with a white ribbon.

The price was reasonable and she would have paid it even if it wasn't. She thanked the clerk, went back out into the heat of the day and followed the familiar route between the church and the fire station. The whole way there she wondered if the raven would put in an appearance, but the only birds she saw were a hawk high up in the northern sky tracing long lazy circles against blue distance, and a few brown sparrows who came out of hiding after the hawk vanished, and started foraging among the weeds on both sides of the old dirt road. None of them followed her into the old cemetery.

The twisted thorn tree over Hepzibah Rewell's grave still had its quota of ribbons hanging in the still air. White for blessings, red for vengeance: Ariel's and Suzanne's ribbons hung a few inches apart, and Ariel nodded, thinking about how they'd both gotten what they'd asked for. It didn't surprise her that there were already flowers on the grave, though she hadn't expected a dozen white roses, real ones, set beside the headstone. Suzanne's doing? It seemed likely enough. Ariel crouched to set her cloth flowers down near the roses, straightened, and stood there looking at the grave for a long moment, thinking of Hepzibah Rewell and Olive Kellinger, and then of Suzanne Kellinger: the witches of Criswell, tracing among them the outlines of a world of magic Ariel had only begun to glimpse.

The Magic Sign? She stifled a laugh. What she'd seen didn't make her special. That much she knew in her bones. She struggled with the thought: it was the world that was more special now that she knew that it had magic in it, somehow, all the way from the vastness of the blue sky overhead, past the faded artificial flowers scattered on the ground, to the centuries-old bones buried down beneath.

"Goody Rewell," she said aloud. "I just wanted to thank you for everything you did. I—" She stopped, because there was nothing else to say. Moments passed, and then she said "Thank you" again and left the cemetery.

The 38 bus hadn't yet left the stop when she returned, so she rode it back through fields and suburbs to the transit mall in downtown Adocentyn, walked from there through summer heat and the long shadows of the golden art deco skyscrapers to her grandfather's house. They had dinner out that night at a little Italian restaurant three blocks away, complete with proper spumoni ice cream for dessert. After that Dr. Moravec buried himself in his study, brooding over strange books written in alphabets Ariel was sure she'd never seen before, while she made another attempt at the book on magic and spent minutes at a time staring past it at nothing in particular, trying to convince herself that her future really had taken so unexpected a turn.

The next morning brought another text from her mother, two screens' worth of irritable words about the lack of a response from Ariel the day before. Ariel deleted it, considered taking the time to send the text she'd drafted a dozen times in her mind the day before, but decided against that. There was a better place and she knew exactly where it was.

Right after breakfast she called Aunt Clarice's shop and got briefly flustered when a younger woman answered the phone. "No, you got the right place," said the voice on the other end, with a broad New Jersey accent. "This is Tasha. 'Pointment for a reading? Yeah, there's still plenty of spots open today." They settled on a time, and Ariel thanked her and hung up.

Outside the weather had turned cooler and big masses of cloud went drifting by, making the sun play hide-and-seek behind them. Ariel headed down Lyon Avenue along a route not quite familiar yet, heading for the old waterfront. That took her down the street lined with bookstores and odd little shops she'd seen on the day she'd given over to tourism—was that really just a week before? The bookshops drew her, though once again she set them aside for later.

An old-fashioned stationery store caught her eye, too: old books she'd read brought to mind notepads in the hands of reporters and detectives, stenographers perched on the edge of desks with spiral-bound tablets open in front of them, file cabinets full of manila folders crammed with clippings and facts. Then, most of the way to the waterfront, she passed a little storefront labeled BILL'S CAMERAS, and the cameras in the window weren't digital. That made her stop and stare for a moment, and then walk on, thinking hard. It had never occurred to her that film cameras might still exist, and once again images from old books came spilling out of memory, bright as flashbulbs going off in her mind.

Another few minutes got her to Harbor Street, where the tourist traps clustered around Duplessy's Museum and the Adocentyn Aquarium. Beyond them, Coopers Bay spread a rumpled silver carpet across to the cranes and container ships of the working waterfront a mile or so away. She grinned as they came into sight. Yes, that was the place.

It was early enough in the day that more than half the tourist restaurants weren't open yet. Ariel had counted on that, and found a little table by Captain Curdie's Fish & Chips next to the railing and the bay. Gulls wheeled around briefly to see if she had any fries to throw them, made off when those weren't forthcoming. She drew in a deep breath of salt-scented air, let it out, got out the cell phone and considered the screen as it woke. Three words, bitter and familiar, murmured themselves in her mind, but she didn't need those now. Her thumbs moved, typing:

MOM AND DAD, IVE GOT WONDERFUL NEWS. I GOT A JOB HERE IN ADOCENTYN. IM GOING TO START WORK NEXT WEEK AS A RESEARCH ASSISTANT FOR ONE OF THE RESEARCHERS AT THE HEYDONIAN INSTITUTION. (That was literally true, she reminded her conscience; they didn't have to know who her boss would be or what kind of research she'd be doing.) IT DOESNT PAY A LOT TO START WITH BUT IT'S ENOUGH FOR ME TO GET BY WHILE I FIGURE OUT WHAT I WANT TO DO WITH MY LIFE. YES I REMEMBER THAT YOU SAID THAT ONCE I LEFT SCHOOL ID HAVE TO PAY MY OWN WAY. IVE THOUGHT ABOUT THAT A LOT AND IM GOOD WITH IT.

One of the seagulls landed on the railing with a flurry of wings and stood there, giving Ariel an expectant look. "Sorry," she told it. "No fries yet." It glared at her, turned its back and walked a few feet along the railing, then spread its wings and soared off.

I KNOW YOU PROBABLY THINK IM MAKING A MISTAKE, she typed then. MAYBE I AM BUT YOU KNOW WHAT, IM GOOD WITH THAT TOO. I KNOW YOU THINK I SHOULD DO THE SAME THING YOU DID WITH YOUR LIVES BUT THATS NOT THE KIND OF LIFE I WANT.

The three words repeated themselves in her mind again. She shoved them aside and kept typing. I LOVE YOU BOTH,

OKAY? IM GLAD YOURE HAPPY WITH YOUR LIVES. I JUST NEED TO DO SOMETHING DIFFERENT WITH MINE. I HOPE YOU AND BRITNEY HAVE AN AMAZING TRIP AND SHE GETS INTO WHATEVER COLLEGE SHE WANTS.

ILL STAY IN TOUCH. ONCE YOU GET BACK HOME YOU CAN PACK UP THE REST OF MY STUFF AND SEND IT TO GRANDPAS PLACE HERE IN ADOCENTYN AND HE CAN GET IT TO ME.

OH YEAH, SOMETHING YOU SHOULD KNOW. THIS PHONE HAS BEEN ACTING UP A LOT LATELY. YOU'D THINK SOMETHING THAT COSTS THIS MUCH WOULD KEEP WORKING LONGER, RIGHT? IF IT GOES OUT IT MAY BE A WHILE BEFORE I CAN AFFORD A NEW PHONE AND I WON'T HAVE THE MONEY FOR A PHONE OR A PLAN THIS FANCY. REMEMBER YOU CAN ALWAYS GET A MESSAGE TO ME THROUGH GRANDPA.

SO THATS THE NEWS. HAVE A WONDERFUL DAY. A

She read the text over once more, made sure everything was the way she wanted it, and then hit SEND. That task done, she got up and walked over to the railing, looked out across Coopers Bay, watched the waves become rippling light as a gap opened up between two masses of cloud and let the sun spill through. A glance at the screen showed her that she had plenty of time to walk back up to Aunt Clarice's shop; two brisk taps turned the phone off.

Then, the act she'd dreamed of for years—

She set the phone on the railing, one end supported by the gray salt-bleached wood, the other over empty air, and rested one hand on each end. A sudden hard pressure, almost a spasm: the phone snapped in half, more easily than she'd expected, though broken electronics behind the screen held the two sides together for the moment. Another quick motion sent the remnants plummeting down into the bay, where it sank with a splash and a few bubbles.

The gap between clouds closed, and Coopers Bay turned the color of hammered silver again. Off the leash once and for all, Ariel turned and started back toward Aunt Clarice's shop.